Black Angels

Also by Rita Murphy

Night Flying

Black Angels

by Rita Murphy

DELACORTE PRESS

Published by
Delacorte Press
an imprint of
Random House Children's Books
a division of Random House, Inc.
1540 Broadway
New York, New York 10036

Visit us on the Web! www.randomhouse.com/kids
Educators and librarians, for a variety of teaching tools, visit us at
www.randomhouse.com/teachers

Library of Congress Cataloging-in-Publication Data

Murphy, Rita.
  Black angels / by Rita Murphy.
    p. cm.
  Summary: The summer of 1961 brings change to eleven-year-old Celli and her town of Mystic, Georgia, when her beloved Sophie becomes involved in the Civil Rights Movement and Celli learns a secret about the father that left her and her family long ago.
  ISBN 0-385-32776-5
  [1. Georgia—Race relations—Fiction. 2. Afro-Americans—Fiction. 3. Racially mixed peoples—Fiction. 4. Civil rights demonstrations—Fiction. 5. Angels—Fiction.] I. Title.

PZ7.M9549 B1 2001
[Fic]—dc21   00-056957

The text of this book is set in 13.25-point Spectrum.

Book design by Alyssa Morris

Manufactured in the United States of America

March 2001

10 9 8 7 6 5 4 3 2 1

BVG

For my parents, Thomas and Mary Murphy

Black Angels

✦ 1 ✦
Angels

Summer 1961

I believe in angels. Black angels. If I come across white angels in a book at the public library, I take out my burnt umber Crayola and cover them in their true skin. I color them all shades of deep brown and black, but my favorite is midnight black. A black so black it is almost blue, like the tar Mama paints on trees in the backyard after a spring storm to stop the open places from bleeding.

I believe in angels because I've seen them. They first appeared to me last month just before school ended. Leaning out the upstairs bathroom window brushing my teeth, I looked down on their heads. Three naked black girls with creamy white wings, throwing stones on my hopscotch board. They had long braided hair that reached to their bottoms. They carried translucent disks that looked like halos under their arms. They giggled to one another and rose up into the crab apple tree, picked blossoms for their hair and flew away.

The angels come every day now since the trouble started. They sit on the barn roof or in the herb garden, eating angel food out of small bundles tied to the end of a stick. They often stay for the afternoon, as long as my dog, Chester, is tied up in the garage. They do not care for Chester. Whenever he sees them or smells their food, he barks until they fly away. He doesn't understand how to behave in the presence of angels and I'm not sure how to teach him.

✦ ✦ ✦

I live in the small town of Mystic, Georgia. "Halfway between somewhere and nowhere," Mama says. A town divided down the center by the Macon County Railway and by the color of people's skin.

I live on the east side of town. The white side.

I never talk about the angels to anyone. I'm afraid there would be trouble if I did. Last summer, Samuel Johnson wandered over from the black side of town and picked some tomatoes out of old Miss Hempstead's garden on Fern Street. They whipped that boy. Sent him back to his mama crying like a baby, though he was almost ten. That's the way it is in Mystic. You have to know where you belong. And the angels belong on the west side of town.

I have one brother. Ellery. He is fourteen years old and has short frizzy brown hair. My daddy had the same kind of hair. Whenever Mama gives me a shampoo, she whispers a sincere prayer of thanks to the Almighty that I was blessed with beautiful Brower hair like her own. Long and dark and wavy.

Ellery usually plays marbles in the driveway before breakfast, but since school ended he's been spending all his time in the garage fixing up an old bicycle his friend Shelby gave him. He has replaced almost every part of it from the brakes to the handlebars. He's trying to turn it into a Bowden Space Lander, which just came off the assembly line this spring and is displayed in the front window of Nickel's Hardware Store. It is the wildest bike I've ever seen. The fenders wrap around it like a skirt and a headlamp in the shape of a cone sprouts from the front of the red fiberglass frame. It's something a spaceman would ride on the moon. How Ellery plans to transform his piece of rusted junk into a sleek, shiny moonbike is beyond me.

He's planning to ride it to the Macon Carnival in August and enter it in a special contest they have there for old bikes made new. I can't imagine anyone getting excited about such a thing, but for the past two weeks it seems to occupy Ellery's every waking moment. Ellery won't let me within ten feet of the garage when he's out there, and when he's not, the bike is covered in old sheets and tucked away in the far corner behind the workbench.

"Celli, you got a match on you?" He calls out of the small open pane on the garage door that he broke with one of his baseballs last week.

"No, Ellery. You know Mama doesn't want you playing with matches."

"Oh, come on, Celli. I got a good reason for wanting it."

"You think you got a good reason, boy," Sophie says, poking her head out the kitchen window. Sophie does the housekeeping and watches us when Mama isn't home. "You children get on in here and eat your grits, or I'm giving you both a bath down in the creek, you hear me?"

Ellery emerges from the garage with a hammer in his hand. "Geez, Celli. You talk so loud. You got a big mouth."

"I do not. You do. I have a beautiful mouth."

"That's right, you tell him, girl." Sophie reaches one arm out the door and grabs a broom off the porch, letting the door snap hard behind her.

Ellery takes off his goggles, closes the garage door and heads up the back steps. I run up behind him, slip under his arm into the kitchen. He swats me with his hand, but it finds only air. Ellery is three years older than I am and although we used to get along when we were little, lately everything I do bothers him and everything he does bothers me.

The kitchen smells like bacon and coffee. Sophie keeps a close eye on Ellery while we eat breakfast to make sure he doesn't have any frogs or snakes in his pockets. He has been known to bring such creatures to the table. When Mama catches him, she calmly tells him to put them on the porch until he is finished eating. Sophie, on the other hand, starts into screaming and makes such a fuss Ellery has to take the critters all the way down to the orchard, which is nearly half a mile from the house, then wash his hands twice before he can come back into *her* kitchen and touch any of *her* food.

Sophie is the biggest, most beautiful black woman I have ever met. She is allowed on the east side of town because Mama hires her. The only reason a black woman would be invited into a white person's house in Mystic is if she's cooking or cleaning for them. That's what Sophie docs for us, plus a whole lot more. Mama says Sophie has been with us so long she's part of the family. She stays with us on Sundays and for the month of July, when Mama goes off to visit our spinster aunt, Etta, up in Atlanta.

"The life of a spinster is a real fine thing, Celli," Mama tells me. She says Etta can move around in as much silence as she pleases, tend her garden without interruption and read a book all morning in bed.

I tell Mama she can stay here and do all those things. Ellery and I will be quiet and she can read anytime she wants to. But she says it's not the same. She says a mama has got to get away once in a while to remember who she is in the world.

Mama has been going to visit Etta every July for the

past ten years. We used to live right next door to Etta with my daddy before he left. In a big old house on Seymour Street, around the corner from the Bubble and Snap, where Daddy played drums every Friday and Saturday night. I don't remember much of that time. I was only one on the night of the big storm when Daddy walked out our front door and never came back.

Mama said Daddy turned at the end of the driveway that night, his white shirt billowing around his tall frame in the wind. He looked right at her and said something, but the rain was so loud on the tin roof above Mama's head she couldn't hear a word. She told me that never in all her life had she so wished she could read lips than on that stormy evening.

"I just sure hope he wasn't telling me he buried a fortune in the basement or left me a bank account under his name in the Atlanta National Bank, 'cause that would be the end of my patience."

I like to imagine he was saying "I love you and I'll be back as soon as I can." But I guess I'll never know for sure.

Mama waited three weeks and when Daddy didn't come back and there were no postcards from a faraway town or envelopes filled with money, she moved us all back to her hometown of Mystic to be closer to Grandma Flo. She took a job at the old folks' home up on the hill overlooking Mystic Country Club. She works every day, wheeling old Mr. Wiley Judson around while he yells out the names of his cows over and over again, and changing diapers. Sometimes when she comes home, she has only enough energy to take off her shoes, throw supper together and cry herself to sleep.

Mama left for Atlanta last Tuesday morning. She packed her bags the night before so everything was ready to go before the sun rose. She'd bought a new summer dress to wear on the train. Bright pink cotton, cut just above the knee.

We were all out in the driveway to say goodbye. Sophie, Ellery, me and my friend Katie Blanchard.

"You look fine, honey," Sophie said, brushing a wisp of hair away from Mama's eyes. "Why, in Atlanta some man might just come along and snatch you right up."

I don't like it when Sophie talks like that. Like someone is going to take Mama away. But Mama just laughed and piled her three suitcases in the trunk of Grandma Flo's shiny new Bel Air station wagon. Grandma Flo waved to me from the driver's side.

"I'll see you on your birthday, honey, after I get back from Vidalia." Grandma Flo was dropping Mama at the station and then heading south for a month to visit her friend Gerty Sanders who had just lost her fourth husband and was in need of a little female companionship. "I'll bring you back some of Gerty's fudge. Be good, now." I gave her a little wave.

Mama kissed Ellery on the forehead and grabbed me up into her arms, lifting me off the ground. She even hugged Katie.

"I'll call once a week to check in. You be good to Sophie, now. Don't give her a hard time," she said, looking mostly at Ellery.

"Don't worry about that," Sophie said. "I'll keep them in line."

Mama started crying then. She always does. "One month," she kept saying to herself, as if it frightened and pleased her at the same time. "In one month you two will have grown three inches on Sophie's cooking." Her mouth turned down into a pout and her eyebrows furrowed. "Why, I don't know if I can leave you both for so long." Mama always wavers at the last minute and Sophie gives me a nudge.

"You go on now, Mama, and have a good time, we'll be just fine," I said, though I didn't feel any such thing. I had secretly been hoping Mama would change her mind about going away and take us all out for ice cream at Wallace's instead. But she slid into the front seat of the station wagon and closed the door.

"Sophie, you got Etta's number, now. You call if you need me, 'cause I can be home within the day. You'll call, now, won't you?" Sophie patted her hand.

"You enjoy yourself, honey, and bring us home some stories."

Mama gave a weak smile and Grandma Flo put the Bel Air in reverse. I stood in the driveway in my white canvas sneakers next to Katie as the car drove down Mariposa

Drive. "One month," I said to myself. "One month is a long time."

✦ ✦ ✦

Sophie has put out two bowls of steaming grits on the table with sour-milk biscuits and elderberry preserves. She's a much better cook than Mama. I wish she could come every day, but Mama says we can't afford Sophie all the time, only on Sundays and in the summer, when help is a necessity.

Halfway through breakfast Chester starts into barking. He's a shaggy white sheepdog who'll bark at almost anything.

"What is ailing that beast?" Sophie wipes her hands on her apron in exasperation and looks out the window. "I swear he's got the hoosamahotchies. Celli, go see to that animal."

It's the angels. Chester is going wild. They must have something good in their bundles today. Something sweet. I lead him to the garage and lock him inside. Then I kneel down in the garden between the sweet potatoes and okra and watch. The angels look beautiful this morning. Their hair catches the light. Their skin glows from the inside out. I have never been able to get too close, maybe twenty feet, before they start to move away. They always seem to know where I am, though they never look in my direction.

No one can see the angels except me and Chester. I've experimented. I've told Sophie to look up at the barn roof when the angels are there and asked Mama if she can see anything unusual in the herb garden, but they just give me an odd look. I'm glad. It's like my own secret, the one thing I have that no one can steal away.

Sometimes after they eat, the angels play marbles or jacks in the dirt beneath the willow tree. Today they dance around the hanging wisps, playing hide-and-seek.

"Honey, what are you doing out there?" Sophie is staring at me from the back porch.

"Nothing," I say.

"Well, that's exactly what it looks like. Did you take care of that beast?"

"I put him in the garage. Something spooked him," I say absentmindedly.

"Get on in here and finish your biscuits, Celli. I got to do up these dishes and get on over to the reverend's."

Sophie belongs to the Reverend Small's gospel church. She takes Ellery and me while Mama works on Sundays. Mama doesn't believe in religion. She says you're more likely to find God up in a sycamore tree than in any old building just 'cause it has a cross on it. She especially does not like the Reverend Small's church. Not because the church is as hot as an oven all months of the year, but because Reverend Small has a way of scaring the hair up on your arms when he speaks. Sophie says that's what she loves about the man. The way his voice can circle up to the roof and fall back down all around you like a good hard spring rain.

"That man's got the Spirit," Sophie says.

I don't spend much time listening to the reverend myself. Lately all he ever talks about is civil rights and the Freedom Riders, who are planning a big rally in Mystic this month. Everyone in the congregation is excited about these folks arriving in buses from the North to speak out against injustice, but I think the whole thing sounds dangerous and I'm tired of listening to the reverend getting all riled up about it. I'd rather look out the window at the trees and daydream. Sophie says that's my problem in a nutshell. She says a child with as little faith as I have should be sitting up in the front row with my ears wide open.

"I do have faith," I tell Sophie. "I have faith in the things I can see." But Sophie says that's no faith at all.

"You got to believe in what you can't see, honey. That's what faith is. You got to know deep in your heart that God answers all prayers. You got to believe. Believing is the hardest part."

I'd like to think the way Sophie does, but I just can't. I've been asking God to send Daddy home ever since I was old enough to understand he was gone and I haven't seen one sign of him yet.

I tell Sophie I prefer to sit in the back row of the reverend's church and watch the folks in the congregation instead. Like Mr. Washington, who turns down his hearing aid and falls asleep as the reverend starts winding up, and the kids who squirm and rustle around so their mamas got to take them outside. The women Sophie's age just stare at Reverend Small as if he were the Almighty Himself come down to take them to the heavenly kingdom. They raise their hands when the reverend pauses to catch his breath and say things like "Yes, Lord. Mmmm. Mmmm. Thank you, Jesus. Thank you," swaying into one another with their eyes closed.

Sophie has been taking us to Screaming River Baptist ever since she started watching us. Ellery and I are about the only white folks in the congregation, but I feel at home there. Some days when Sophie gets us to church early, I play jacks with Tilly and Rosa Johnson out under the persimmon tree. Tilly always wins. She's the best jacks player I know and Rosa makes pretty little dolls out of the bell-shaped persimmon flowers when they're in bloom.

During service I usually sit between Sophie and Bertha, Tilly and Rosa's mama. Sophie says it is not a good idea to let three giggly girls sit next to one another in church.

Ellery usually sits behind us next to Fergus Freeman. Fergus is a friend of ours, though Ellery won't admit it. Ellery might spend time with Fergus on Sundays, but he thinks he's too cool to have anyone know he's friends with a black person. He and Fergus play ball with George and Arlo Jackson after service out in the field behind the church. Fergus is a lefty and so is Ellery. I know Ellery likes Fergus like I like Tilly and Rose. But we rarely see each other outside of service. Not even in the summer. They're our Sunday friends.

Once in a blue moon Fergus comes over to our house to run an errand for Sophie, but he'll never stay long even if Sophie invites him to sit down for dinner. It seems like the only place we all feel relaxed enough to be with each other is at church.

It doesn't seem to bother anyone at Screaming River Baptist that I'm a different color. They just call me So-phie's girl. I know it's because I'm still young that I can go with Sophie. When I turn twelve next summer, I proba-bly won't be able to come anymore. I'll have to go to church with Grandma Flo. I've seen it happen before.

Missy Bender came to church with her maid, Shirley, every Sunday for years. Then Missy turned thirteen last May and started filling out the top of all her Sunday dresses and the boys in the congregation looked at her differently. Sophie and the ladies of the choir had a meet-ing and the next week Missy Bender was no longer a member of our congregation. I've seen her since, walking to the big white church in the center of town where Grandma Flo took me once. Nothing exciting happens in there. No one stands up and shouts out the name of the Lord inside those big white walls or gets up in the aisles to dance. Everyone sits politely in the dark, polished pews and takes note of what other folks are wearing, and the minister talks about money. I have to believe that there is a way around all of this. Maybe if I stay small and skinny and never grow any breasts, then I can keep coming with Sophie forever.

My favorite part of the service is when Reverend Small stops preaching and the choir sings. There are five women in the choir. Five women with voices rich like cream. When they sing "Amazing Grace" at the end of each service, I get the feeling I might cry or shout or raise my arms above my head the way Sophie does. Their voices crawl into a lonely place inside my chest just above my ribs, the place that gets bigger after Mama leaves for the summer, and while I'm listening it doesn't ache anymore. Feels like someone just poured warm, sweet honey down inside and filled it to the brim.

I used to look for the angels in church, thinking it might be a place they'd want to visit. But they've never come. I imagine since their ears are extra-sensitive, it might be too much for them when the reverend gets going.

Sophie has never missed a Sunday service at Screaming River Baptist in the ten years I have known her, which means Ellery and I have never missed one either, except for that week I went to church with Grandma Flo. Sophie takes us even if we're sick. That's her way. She never asks us what we want to do. She tells us.

"We're going over to clean the church," she'll say, or

"Mrs. Gains on the county road just had her fifth child and we're bringing her a pan of corn bread."

If you try to protest, she'll give you a good long lecture on the meaning of the word *neighborly* and shake her head.

"You white folks got nothing to bind you together. That's the problem. When times get hard you all just go it alone or stuff it in the kitchen closet with the brooms. Lord, Jesus, what a sorrowful lot."

This is the way Sophie speaks. I'm used to it and sometimes what she says makes sense to me, but other white folks won't hire Sophie 'cause they say she's got trouble written all over her sassy face. I love Sophie's face.

I once met Sophie's granny Rose, who is ninety-six. A tiny, brittle woman who hardly says a word and whose skin is so light she looks a lot like my aunt Etta, who sits out in the sun all day long. I worry sometimes that this might happen to Sophie when she grows old—that she'll shrivel and lose all her color—but Sophie assures me the Lord gave her enough color to last two lifetimes.

I've come to think that if there is a God, she probably looks a lot like Sophie. A big, black, bossy woman with sturdy arms that could wrap around me twice. A woman who will wipe the dirt from my face with her own spit, scold me for forgetting my manners and then gather me in her lap and sing me gospel songs until I fall asleep.

I love to sit on the heater in the kitchen and watch Sophie while she cooks. Her face gets all shiny from the heat, especially in July, when the temperature in the house can go over one hundred. She smells like cherries and onions, which is kind of sweet or sour depending on the day.

Her hands are wide but gentle. And every once in a while if she's resting or shelling peas on the porch, she'll reach over and fluff up my hair with her gentle hand and shake her head. "Celli, you got a bit of the angels about you, girl."

✦ **2** *✦*
The Letter

My full name is Celline Brower Jenkins. I am the only girl on the Jenkins side of the family. According to Mama, all of my father's brothers and uncles, grandfathers and great-grandfathers going back twelve generations have produced boys. I am a freak of nature. Mama says not to give it a second thought. It's better to be a girl. The Jenkins men, she says, are good at passing down the family name. They're just not so good about staying around to see how it all comes out.

I have one picture of my daddy on the mirror over my bureau. He is tall and lanky and looks just like Ellery would if Ellery had a beard. Mama says she thinks Daddy lives near Atlanta now, but she's not sure.

"Why don't you go look for him?" I asked her once.

"I can't do that, Celli."

"Why not?" I persisted. "Why can't you just find him and bring him on home?"

"Because, honey, he doesn't want to come home."

I always hope that Mama will see Daddy one day on her vacation and he'll fall in love with her all over again and come home to us. But that hasn't happened yet.

My only memory of my daddy is of being on top of his shoulders at the Macon Carnival one summer. Mama said I was not even one at the time so there is no way I could remember such a thing, but I do. I dropped ice cream in his hair and he laughed and twirled me up near the lights of the Ferris wheel and kissed me on the forehead. If I sit real quiet on the edge of the windowsill in my bedroom while it's raining, I think I can smell him again. A clean, woody smell mixed with fried-pepper sandwiches and cotton candy.

Mama says her biggest mistake in life was getting involved with a musician. My daddy was a drummer.

"The life of a musician is hard, Celli. Up at all hours, drinking, smoking. Not a good life. Your daddy tried, but it was hard for him to be with one woman for very long."

Mama met Daddy while visiting Aunt Etta in Atlanta one summer. She was eighteen, he was thirty. He'd come down from Ohio to play his drums in a band called the Blue Shoes. Mama went out with some friends one Saturday night to the Bubble and Snap and Daddy was playing.

Mama said the minute she walked in, she caught sight of him and couldn't take her eyes off his hands, moving like lightning over the surface of the drums. After the band finished Daddy asked Mama out for a stroll around Thayer Park and she accepted. "Love at first sight" was what she said.

Mama has a wedding photo on her bureau of the two of them on the boardwalk in Savannah, where they ran away to get married. Grandma Florence did not approve. She said it would last two weeks.

"It lasted four years," Mama proudly reminds her.

Just enough time to bring me and Ellery into the world, which Mama says has been the greatest blessing of all.

Grandma Flo lives up near the country club in the big old mansion on First Street where Mama grew up. She wanted us all to come live with her when we first came back from Atlanta, but Mama said returning to her hometown as a grown woman was hard enough, she didn't want to go living in her mother's house besides. Mama lets Grandma Flo pay for Sophie, but that's all. The rest she does herself. She doesn't like to be beholden to anyone, not even her own mother. Mama says it's easier to live in Mystic if she has her own life. Because we live in our own house, Grandma Flo doesn't try to tell Mama what to do anymore, especially since Daddy left.

Maybe it was my daddy's occupation that set Grandma

Flo off, but she never liked him. Being a drummer, Daddy was always tapping his foot on the porch floor or rapping his fork against Grandma Flo's fine crystal water pitcher, and it got on her nerves. But Mama says that's what made her fall in love with Daddy in the first place. She says Daddy had a beat inside him that would not quit and her heart just had to beat with it. He was not a handsome man. He was not daring or mysterious. Mama says he was plain ordinary and a little on the homely side, to be perfectly honest, but a great kisser.

"Maybe that's what it was, Celli. Maybe I got all wound around your daddy because of his lips. Your daddy sure had a fine set of lips."

Mama is not shy about telling me such things. She says she wants me to know so one day I can make up my own mind what I want when I'm a grown woman. Mama says "Marry a man who can be your friend."

I'll be twelve years old in August. Since my birthday always falls on the hottest day of the year, Sophie says she has no intention of ever baking me a cake. Instead, every year we take out the old ice cream maker from the second floor of the garage and stir up a batch of Strawberry Ecstasy. Sophie pours a little rum in on the side. That's what gives it the ecstasy. I'm not supposed to mention this fact to Reverend Small. Sophie says if I do, she'll never cook for me again and I'll have to eat my eggs raw and my grits straight out of the sack.

Mama always comes home on my birthday and after she hugs Ellery and me and gives me my present, which usually consists of a pound of Etta's butterscotch fudge and a pretty cotton dress, she and Sophie sit out on the veranda for hours, laughing and slapping their knees.

"Lawd, Sophie, I sure am glad to see you," Mama says, and they hug each other like sisters who haven't seen each other in a century.

Then they always have a homecoming drink—an eighth of a glass of brandy—plus a plate of cucumber sandwiches and catch up on the adventures of the summer.

Mama does all the talking, which is unusual since Sophie is the one who usually talks your ear off. Mama will be all trim and tan, her thick dark hair in a stylish flip. You'd never know she just got off a train. She likes to wear pillbox hats and pumps, bright-colored shirtwaist dresses and perfume. To see her sitting next to Sophie, you wouldn't think they're the same age, but they are. Sophie says Mama goes out and lives life in the summer for both of them and fills her in later on so Sophie gets to see what a great summer she's had after all.

Sophie has never been outside the town line of Mystic. She lives on a road that has no name. White folks sometimes call it Shanty Road, as that is what used to line both sides of it—wood and tar paper shacks separated by broken board fencing. It's not like that anymore, though. Most of Sophie's neighbors live in small wood-frame houses with gardens out back. No white folks ever go there, but they still call it Shanty Road anyway.

"That's typical," Sophie says. "Don't want us black folks thinking too highly of ourselves for having running water. Might get it into our heads to ride in the front of the bus next." It does sound silly, but some white folks think there are still shacks out there.

My friend Katie Blanchard told me if you walk down Shanty Road at midnight, your skin will turn black and you'll have to stay there forever and live in the same house with your chickens. Katie laughed when she said that, though I didn't find it funny.

Mama told me igorance is what turns people hard against each other because of the way they look or where they live. "They've just forgotten, Celli. That's all. If folks could love everything about themselves, then they'd have no need to make distinctions. The color of a person's skin is a beautiful thing, whatever color it is."

I have only been to Sophie's Road once—that's what I call it. Sophie had the flu last summer and Mama and I brought her a pot of melon soup and a huckleberry pie. Sophie loves huckleberries and last summer the huckleberries were so plentiful they were dripping off the bushes. We didn't go inside Sophie's house. She wouldn't let us in the front door—didn't want us to catch her germs—so we just left everything on the front stoop. I'd like to go inside Sophie's house one day, sit down at the table and eat grits with her. I'd like to run down Sophie's Road at midnight just to see what happens.

✦ ✦ ✦

Wednesday is baking day. The house smells of pecans. Sophie has been known to turn out six pecan pies before nine A.M. Enough for every member of the congregation who is in need and one left over for her granny Rose, who practically lives on sweet potatoes and pies. But this morning Sophie only needed to make one pie, for the Reverend Small's wife, who is feeling poorly because of the heat.

At ten o'clock, Sophie shoos Ellery and me to the car. Mama takes the train to Atlanta so we can have the Dodge Dart. The Dart once belonged to Grandma Flo, but now it belongs to us since she bought herself that brand-new station wagon. The Dart is small compared to the Oldsmobile we used to have and whenever Sophie drives it, I have to scoot over toward the door to give her enough elbowroom. Sophie hates to feel cramped and in that car it's mighty hard not to.

We drive out the old turnpike road to the Screaming River. Sophie says it's called that because a bunch of old swampers got stuck down there and drowned during the flood of '34. "That's what you're hearin'," she'll say when the wind blows just right and the high-pitched moan rises up through the cypress trees. "They're screaming for their salvation. They're repentin' for all the drinkin' and cussin' and cheatin' they done when they was alive."

Mama says that's just old superstition. There's nothing down there but a narrow tunnel of roots that the wind gets stuck in sometimes, like a cork in a bottle. When the pressure builds up, it comes out sounding kind of ghostly, but it's nothing but the wind all along. Ellery and I tend to side with Sophie on this matter. There is something about the sound that's so close to a human cry of pain I know it's got to be more than the wind.

The Screaming River Baptist Church sits on the edge of the Screaming River, about five miles outside the town line of Mystic. It is a little square box painted white with a black cross perched on the top like a weather vane. The inside is plain, with six rows of wooden chairs and a pulpit up front. Reverend Small isn't there today, for which I am grateful. I like the reverend. He's a kind man and always shakes my hand after service and asks after Mama. But next to preaching, the best thing the reverend does is talk. When he and Sophie get going, Ellery and I can go through two pitchers of lemonade and a whole plate of Mrs. Small's oatmeal cookies with time to spare.

Today Mrs. Small is the only one home. She is truly small, unlike the reverend who is as big as a bear. She is so thin you can see the bones of her wrists poking through the cuffs of her shirt. Sophie says she isn't well, never has been, is of delicate constitution. She reminds me of Lot's wife in the Bible, who was turned into a pillar of salt—kind of chalky and dried-up, as if the Georgia sun has evaporated all of her bodily juices. She is a quiet woman and politely thanks Sophie for the pie. After Sophie asks about her health and the reverend's sermon for the coming week, we say goodbye and pile back in the car.

"Lord have mercy, she's a strange one," Sophie says as she slides herself behind the steering wheel. "Getting any stories out of that woman is like trying to squeeze water from a stone."

Stories of the congregation is what Sophie means. Sophie usually can't wait until Sunday service to find out what's happening. Did someone die or have a baby? These are things Sophie needs to know.

"We're going home a different way today," Sophie tells us. She drives down the turnpike, cuts across the parkway through town to the corner of Elm and State where the courthouse is. The same group of folks with signs is standing on the courthouse steps that has been there all week. Sophie parks across the street and shuts off the engine. She slips off her shoes, bends down and rubs her feet. Sophie's feet bother her a lot. Mama says she should wear special shoes to support them, but Sophie just laughs. "Where you gonna get special shoes for feet as big as mine?" she always asks. So instead of buying new ones, she wears her old flats with the broken heels during the week and her good shoes on Sundays. The soles of the old shoes are so thin Sophie says she can sometimes feel the heat of the pavement right through them, and the good Sunday shoes are too tight. So either way Sophie has to sit down to rest as often as possible.

Sophie puts her feet up on the seat next to me and we watch the folks outside the courthouse. Some are white and some are black. Most I've never seen before. The signs they carry are lifted high up on wooden sticks and say things like Freedom for All and We Shall Overcome.

"More people from the North will be coming soon and the white folks are getting jumpy," Sophie says, nodding her head in the direction of a small group of men hanging around on the corner watching the protesters. My stomach tightens a little at the sight of them. The way they glance over at the folks carrying signs looks anything but friendly.

"At the mass meeting last Wednesday night, the reverend told us to prepare ourselves for a storm. He said that even though all we plan on doing is marching from the bus station to the courthouse and giving a few speeches, we should expect trouble. He preached for close to an hour and when he was done Halia Monroe sang 'Didn't My Lord Deliver Daniel.' By the end, everyone in that room would have walked through fire for the Movement."

Even though I wish Sophie weren't involved with the

Freedom Movement, listening to her talk about the meetings makes me want to go to one myself just to see what it's like. But Sophie won't take me and Ellery. She says they go on too late and since she's busy organizing the whole thing with Reverend Small, she doesn't have time to keep a proper eye on us.

"Every Negro in this town has got to stand up this summer. We've been sitting around too long. This is our moment to stand together and we can't let it pass us by. Not this time."

Sophie goes on like this whenever she talks about the Movement. She could spend all afternoon talking and forget to take a breath. On more than one occasion she has worked herself into a full-fledged speech lasting more than an hour, after which Ellery and I applaud and whistle.

"We know," Ellery says, spitting out a wad of chewing gum and fastening it to the vinyl under his seat. He has a whole collection going under there. "We've heard it all before, Sophie. The Negroes got to stand up."

"You don't know nothing, Mister Smartpants," Sophie says, turning around in her seat. "You'd stand right up there with us if you had a brain inside that head of yours or one single bone of courage."

It surprises me how Ellery will try to get Sophie going only to have Sophie shut him up the minute he gets started. Sophie's tongue, unlike her body, is as fast as a whip. She wins every argument. If Sophie were a white woman, I wouldn't worry about her talking so freely, but going on like she does is downright dangerous for a black woman in a town like Mystic. Even Reverend Small says Sophie's tongue is one of her greatest gifts to the Movement and one of his worst nightmares.

I sit in the garden for most of the afternoon, pulling weeds for Sophie. She gives me a large coffee can filled with kerosene to collect potato bugs in, but so far I haven't seen any. Even if I do find some, I won't put them in the can. I'll take them down to the creek and let them go in the sand. I feel differently about bugs than Sophie does. I have no need to do away with them just because they're in the wrong place.

At noon Mr. Pearson walks up the porch steps and clanks the mailbox lid, slides in a bundle and continues on.

"Celli, you staying out of trouble?" he inquires. He always asks the same thing when he delivers our mail.

"Yes sir, Mister Pearson. Nothing to get into trouble with around here."

"That's a good girl, Celli. You keep it that way."

I run to the mailbox and leaf through the bundle. Bills and a Sears, Roebuck catalog for Mama, a letter for Mama, a package for Ellery from the Bionic Book Club, a postcard from Mama in Atlanta saying she arrived safely and one letter for Ellery and me.

Celline and Ellery Jenkins
324 Mariposa Drive
Mystic, Georgia

The writing is tiny and scrawled and bumpy, like someone wrote it while riding on the back of a horse.

I hardly ever receive a letter except near my birthday.
Maybe it was delivered wrong. But there's my name next
to Ellery's as clear as day. I figure since my name is first, I
have the right to open it. I rip off one end like I've seen
Mama do and blow inside, puffing up the white paper,
turn it upside down and give a shake. A thin, folded piece
of stationery falls out onto the porch. I pick it up and un-
fold it.

Dear Celline and Ellery,

*My name is Pearl Jenkins. I live in Cleveland, Ohio. I am
your daddy's mama. Your grandmother. I met you both once when
you were very young. I would like to meet you again now that you
are grown. I am planning on coming through Mystic on the
weekend of July 15th. I will be staying at the Horn Motor Lodge
out on the turnpike. I have also written a letter to your mama
telling her of my visit and desire to meet you. I hope that you will
join me for lunch at the Elgin Hotel on July 16th at noon.*

Love,

Grandma Pearl

Something jumps up and down in my belly. Like one of those little wooden men, jointed with string, who fall into a heap when you press the button at the bottom of their stand. I sit down in the white wicker porch chair and read the letter again. Grandma Pearl. I never thought I had another grandma besides Grandma Flo. Mama has never mentioned her. Maybe if she really is my grandma, then she knows where Daddy lives. Maybe he lives with her and wants to see me too. I start running through my mind all the summer dresses I have hanging in my closet. I'll wear the yellow one with lavender flowers and I'll let my hair fall down loose and dab on a drop of Mama's peach blossom perfume. Or maybe I'll wear the purple silk dress Aunt Etta sent for Christmas. I'll arrive right before noon and we'll greet one another on the front stairs. She'll be an elegant woman with short white hair, like Bobbie Orkin's grandmother who comes down from New York every spring with parcels of chocolates and hair ribbons. We'll have lunch on the Elgin's white tablecloths and she'll tell me all about her life in Ohio and I'll tell her all about mine.

I sift through Mama's mail and sure enough there is a letter from Pearl. I take both letters and fold them in half, slide them into the pocket of my overalls. I'm *not* going to show Ellery. He'd just ruin Grandma Pearl's visit. I want to meet her on my own first. It's more important to me than it is to Ellery anyway. He doesn't even like going out to lunch. And if he did go, he might say something stupid. I'll keep my letter with me for the next two weeks directly on my person and I'll give Mama her letter myself when she comes home. Sophie opens all Mama's mail for her while she's away and if Sophie reads this letter, she might not let me go or she'll want to come with me. And I have every intention of going alone.

✦ 3 ✦
Quilting

This morning the angels come in from the west. They are wearing sneakers and all three have disks under their arms. I don't know what these are used for. Occasionally one of the angels will take hers out and twirl it between her hands, lift it to the center of her chest, close her eyes as if in prayer.

I'm not sure why the angels come. They never speak to me, but somehow their presence fills me with hope. Whenever I see them descending into the peach trees or sitting in the garden, I don't feel alone and the month of July doesn't seem so long. Sophie told me that if you know you're not alone, if there are folks around you who love you, then you can do just about anything in life. You can even do things that frighten you. If there is just one person in the world who truly sees you, it can make all the difference. I think I know what she means, because I feel this way when the angels are around. Like they're keeping an eye on me.

It is early July and the magnolia trees are covered with white blossoms. The yard smells sweet, as if someone just dumped a whole canister of pure cane sugar over everything. It makes me feel dizzy, breathing in all that sweetness. I sit on the last step of the porch, wipe my nose on my sleeve and watch the angels.

They are rebraiding each other's hair. I've seen them do this before. Sometimes they'll take one skinny long braid apart and fix it. First they comb out the hair with branches from the peach trees. Combing, combing until all the snarls have been worked out. Then they weave slowly and evenly until the braid hangs in a long skinny rope down their back with all the other little braids.

The angels' hair is not like Sophie's hair, which never grows more than a quarter of an inch a year. It is more like the hair of Yemaya, the beautiful black mermaid who lives under the sea. Sophie told me the story of Yemaya once. How she comes to the surface of the water when you call her name and grants you three wishes if your heart is pure. Sophie said Yemaya's hair hangs in long braided locks down her back. I guess hair must grow faster under the sea and in heaven.

Chester is over at the Harveys' sniffing around the

compost, so the angels stay. They pull out their bundles and settle down to sandwiches and long strings of food that look like pearls. They feed these strands to one another while balancing little jam tarts on the tips of their fingers.

I reach into the front pocket of my overalls and pull out the letter from Grandma Pearl. I like the sound of her name. *Pearl. Pearl. Pearl.* Like a shiny white bead. Like a treasure hidden deep in the ocean you've spent your whole life trying to find. *Pearl. Pearly. The pearly gates. A pearl of great price.*

Ping! I am jolted from my thoughts by the sound of a beebee hitting metal. I duck my head and turn in the direction of the noise. Ellery is practicing with his gun against a target on the back of the house. Sophie doesn't want him to do that when I'm around. She's afraid he'll put my eye out with that thing. But Sophie is down in the basement with the washing machine going and when Sophie's doing laundry, she can't hear anything softer than a scream and Ellery knows it.

Ping! Ping! Two more beebees bounce off the metal watering can. I suck in my breath and Ellery hears me. Turns in my direction. He points the gun directly at my chest.

"Stop it, Ellery," I shout.

"Stop it, Ellery," he mimics me. "Aw, you're not worth shooting," he laughs. "Too skinny." He leans the gun against the house and moves toward the garden. I silently fold up the letter and am about to slip it back into my pocket when Ellery runs up and snatches it out of my hands.

"Whatcha got there, Celli?"

"Ellery, give that back or you're in big trouble." Ellery dances around with the letter high over his head. *Please,* I think, *don't let him see his name.*

"If you don't give it to me right now, Ellery, I'm gonna scream. I'm gonna scream so loud and so bad, Sophie will wring your neck before she asks questions. You know I will, Ellery, and you'll get no supper tonight."

Ellery continues to dance around.

Out of the corner of my eye I can see the angels packing up their food. Ellery has scared them away again. He has a habit of showing up at the wrong time with his bee-bee gun or some noisy machine that sends the angels flying off faster than I can count to ten. Today, though, they move away slowly. One of the angels, the tallest of the three, pulls a small cake out of her bundle and holds it up to the wind. From the direction of the Harveys', Chester catches the scent and comes running. Chester is fat, dirty and full of fleas because Sophie refuses to wash him in the summer and Ellery and I have better things to do than spend an entire day trying to convince him to sit in a tub of suds and let us spray him with a hose. By August he ends up a deep shade of brown, though underneath he's as white as my teeth. Chester comes bounding over the pea fence straight for the little cake, which is right above

Ellery's head, and knocks him flat on the ground. I race over and grab the letter, which catches in the tendrils of the sugar peas. I fold it quickly and stuff it in my undershirt.

"Chester, you stinking dog, get off me."

I laugh as Ellery tries to pry Chester's dirty paws off his chest. The angels begin to lift off and I smile at them. The tallest angel winks at me, puts her bundle over her shoulder and disappears above the trees.

After supper Sophie asks me to come sit out on the porch with her while Ellery does the dishes.

"I need your help with something, Celli."

"What is it?" Ellery asks.

"None of your business, Mister Ellery. You keep those dishes moving, you hear?"

On the porch, next to the wicker rocker, there is a big cloth bag filled with scraps of fabric. I saw Sophie carrying it down from the attic before supper.

"What's it for?" I ask.

"A quilt," Sophie says, easing herself into a chair and rummaging through the bag. "I'm making a quilt for your mama's bed."

"Mama's already got the quilt Grandma Flo made for her."

"Well, this is gonna be different. This is like the quilt my people make. I been saving scraps of your pajamas and

Ellery's shirts for three years and I think it's about time your mama sees what we do here all summer. It ain't gonna be a big quilt, as we don't do nothing big. Just a little one to put on her lap or hang on the wall behind her bed. And you're gonna help me."

"I don't even know how to sew, Sophie."

Sophie shakes her head in disapproval and I hear her tongue clicking against the roof of her mouth.

"We got to teach you one useful thing, girl, before we send you out into the world. Sit down here," she says, patting the seat of the chair next to her.

Sophie pulls out two squares of fabric. One from my old pink church dress and a pocket from Ellery's green pants. Sophie shows me how to thread a needle without pricking my finger, then pokes the needle down into the fabric and pulls it up and through. I've seen her do it before. I saw Mama fix the strap on her slip one time, too, but I've never sewn anything myself.

After a few tries of poking my fingers, I start to get into a little rhythm. When we hear Ellery finish the last pan and run upstairs and shut the door behind him, Sophie puts her sewing down on her lap and watches me. She hums a little and rocks back in her chair.

"Celli," she says, rocking forward and stopping with her chin almost in my lap. "I got to ask you a question. You don't got to answer it if you don't want to and if I'm prying you tell me."

My heart starts jumping. She knows about Grandma Pearl's letter! I suck in my breath, my hands stop the pushing and pulling of thread. I look up into her deep brown eyes. Eyes like the pools flowing into the Screaming River.

"What do you do out in the garden when you just sit there? Are you praying?"

I just stare at her and begin breathing again.

" 'Cause that's what it looks like to me. Like you're praying."

I don't say anything.

"I seen Addy Smith at the Grace Baptist Church. Addy's got the Spirit. This look comes over her face like the look that comes over yours in the garden and she starts speaking in tongues and falls over backwards." Sophie stops talking and rocks back in her chair.

I'm just busting inside 'cause there is a part of me wants to tell Sophie everything and yet I'm afraid if I do the angels will stop coming. I have this idea in my head that if you love something, you got to keep it close to you, be real quiet about it and not tell a soul or else it'll be taken away. I'm not exactly sure where this idea came from. Maybe it's because of something Mama said to me once about how much she loved Daddy and then one day he got up and went away forever. I've been keeping things I love to myself ever since, just to be on the safe side.

"I'm going to tell you a story, Celli," Sophie says, settling herself into a steady rocking. "When I was your age I used to be real sad. I always been big. A big fat girl," she laughs. "A big fat girl with one tooth stuck straight out like a divining rod from my mouth. I didn't have but one friend, my old rooster, Gordon, and when Gordon died, I had none at all. I never had much family except for Granny Rose and my sister, Jo. I went to work when I was younger than you, ironing for the white folks.

"Some said it was that one crooked tooth that turned everything I said into trouble. My Granny Rose called it the 'tooth of truth,' as that was what came out of my mouth, the truth of how I see things. Well, I learned young that telling the truth in this town ain't nothing but a dangerous game, so I tried to keep my lips over that tooth most of the time. One day it just up and fell out all on its own, but by then it was too late. Left me with the curse of never letting anything go by me without saying my piece. That's how I come to work for your mama. She don't mind listening to my talk."

Sophie rocks a little slower. Her eyes sink way back in her head, like she's trying to see something a long way off.

"There was a time, though, before I started working for your mama, when not a soul would hire me. I lived with Granny Rose and Jo and for six whole months we ate nothing but red beans and rice and sour apples.

"One night as I was falling off to sleep with my stomach empty, I seen something in the doorway of my room. I can't tell you exactly what it was. It stayed only a minute. A bright light that hurt my eyes. Granny Rose didn't see it, but she believed me when I told her the next morning. She said she felt a presence in the house that night and she knew things were gonna change. Two days later, your mama moved back into town. She was desperate for help while she looked for work and didn't mind about my reputation. She hired me on the spot to watch after you and that brother of yours. Though I'm not sure if you'd call that a miracle, having to watch over two children don't know the difference between peas and carrots." She gives me a wink. "I was mighty grateful at the time, let me tell you that. Still can't look at a sour apple without my stomach turning." She laughs, taking two more squares from the scrap bag.

"I come to feel, Celli, that that light was an angel come down to remind me that I never have to do this life alone."

I look up from my sewing. Look directly at Sophie. Take a deep breath, 'cause I'm not exactly sure what's gonna come out.

"That's a real interesting story, Sophie," I say, "but I don't see nothing in the garden 'cept what's there. I got a tendency to daydream is all. Mama says so herself. She says that's the one thing I'm best at."

I bend my head down over my sewing to end the conversation. I love Sophie and I would tell her most anything. But I can't tell her about the angels. I need them to keep coming around. Out of the corner of my eye I notice Sophie put down her piece real quiet and a smile turn up the corners of her mouth.

Pennies

Katie Blanchard is taking me to town today for a malt at Wallace's and a movie at the Savoy Theater. *Sabrina* is playing, with Audrey Hepburn and Humphrey Bogart. Ellery and his friend Shelby Daniels saw it yesterday and Ellery said it was a sissy girl movie so we should like it.

In Ellery's opinion there are only two kinds of movies. Sissy girl movies, which means there is some kind of kissing in them, and real movies, which means there is some kind of fighting in them. Ellery has been to every western ever shown at the Savoy in the past two years. He likes to act tough like John Wayne.

Over the workbench in the garage, Ellery has pasted up a picture of "The Duke." It takes up half the wall. I caught Ellery posing beside it once when I walked in to get some canning jars for Sophie. He had his thumbs tucked into his belt and he was staring down the lawn mower. Just him and John Wayne, waiting to see who would draw first. Maybe that's what Ellery thinks about men. That they have to be tougher than Daddy was. Tough enough to stick around.

Shelby and Ellery have been in the garage sorting through boxes since sunup. Shelby whispers something in Ellery's ear and Ellery laughs. "Yeah, they'll love that movie," he says, making kissing noises loud enough for Katie and me to hear.

"Maybe you'll get to sit next to your boyfriend, Jimmy Bottlebrain," Shelby says.

"Be quiet, Shelby," says Katie. "You don't know anything. You're just jealous Jimmy's on the football team and you're too little to even try out." Shelby's face turns red.

Shelby is too small to play football or any other sport. Too short and pudgy to even walk the length of the playing field, let alone run it. Everybody knows Shelby's daddy wanted him to be a football star from the moment of his birth. He bought Shelby a uniform and everything, but no matter how hard you try to stretch it, Shelby's just not built for sports.

"Come on, Katie, let's go." I pull her toward the sidewalk. "He can't help it he's small," I whisper. Katie just shrugs her shoulders.

"Then he shouldn't say anything about Jimmy Bottle."

Katie has a crush on Jimmy Lee Bottle worse than I've ever seen, but I don't think he even remembers her name unless she reminds him, which she does whenever she sees him. "Hi, Jimmy," she'll say with a big wide grin. "It's me, Katie Jolene Blanchard!" She'll wave at him until he says hello or walks away. Katie is not easily discouraged in matters of the heart. She cut out Jimmy's picture from the yearbook and pasted it to the mirror above her bureau. She even has a votive candle lit underneath it, like a shrine. The Jimmy Bottle shrine, I call it, but Katie doesn't mind. She's in love and doesn't care who knows it.

Jimmy Lee Bottle will be a senior in high school this fall, which means he is five years older than we are. He is captain of the football team. His daddy, Thomas Bottle, owns the Emery Bank and his uncle Frank owns the five-and-dime. Katie says she's gonna marry Jimmy one day and who knows, maybe she will. Katie usually gets whatever she wants.

It is because of Katie Jolene Blanchard that I can go to the movies at all. Mama usually doesn't have enough loose change lying around to send me on my own, so Katie treats me. Her daddy runs the quarry east of town and they have loads of money, so I let her. I like going to the movies, but sometimes I wish I could go with Tilly and Rosa instead, though that's not as simple as it seems. They'd have to sit up in the colored balcony and I'd sit downstairs with the other white folk. And we couldn't sit together at the lunch counter at Wallace's afterward and eat ice cream either. It's against the rules and besides, Katie and her friends would tease me no end for being seen with colored girls. It's too bad, because they're much more fun than Katie is and don't talk about themselves near as much.

Katie and I walk down Main Street to Wallace's, where Jimmy works in the summer. Katie wants to buy a book of stamps and watch Jimmy from behind one of the shelves before we sit down for a malt. In my opinion, Katie wastes a lot of her time spying on Jimmy when she could just walk right up and talk to him. But Katie prefers to watch him when he doesn't know she's looking. Not because she's shy, but because she says she wants to observe him in his natural state.

Jimmy is cleaning behind the soda counter when we walk in, but he doesn't see us. He is tall and thin with a little stubble of beard on his chin. He has cold blue eyes, dirty blond hair and a permanent smirk on his face. I overheard Ellery tell Shelby one day that all the Wallaces and Bottles belong to the Klan. Ellery used to play with Jimmy's younger brother, Ned, and one afternoon Ned showed Ellery the cabinet where his father kept his gun and his white hooded robe. Ellery has heard far too many stories from Sophie about the Klan and I think something about that robe scared him, 'cause he never went back to play at the Bottles' house again. Sophie says that the Klan is just a bunch of cowards running around in nightgowns, so ashamed of their own hatred they have to cover their faces with hoods. Somehow it's not hard for me to imagine Jimmy in one of those robes.

"There he is," Katie whispers, grabbing my arm and pulling me behind a rack of hair bands. "Isn't he beautiful? Isn't he the most beautiful man you've ever seen?"

"He isn't a man, Katie," I remind her. "He's still in high school and he doesn't even have a full beard yet."

Katie doesn't pay any attention. She stares at Jimmy. Then just as quickly she turns around and picks up a magazine, pretending to look through it, pointing out an advertisement to me for men's cotton briefs. "Oh, Celli, don't you think that's lovely?" she asks, her voice all high and dreamy. I don't understand what she's doing until Jimmy walks by us and Katie glances up. "Hi, Jimmy," she says. He turns around. "Oh, hi," he replies, not even breaking stride.

"Did you hear him, Celli? He said hi to me!"

"Yeah, Katie, I heard him." I leave Katie to spy on Jimmy and I head for a little shelf of books at the rear of the store. I've been waiting a full month for the new *Jackson Quarterly* to come out and there it is right in the front. It's full of mystery stories and poetry. It costs two dollars and fifty cents. I have only one dollar and thirty-five cents in the sock in the top drawer of my bureau at home. I hope this copy stays around long enough for my birthday to come, so I can ask Mama for it.

"Lord have mercy, don't tell me I can't sit here." I whirl around at the sound of Sophie's voice. I peek through the shelves of books toward the checkout at the front of the store. Sophie is sitting at the soda counter looking Jimmy Bottle hard in the eye. Katie sneaks up behind me.

"It's Sophie," I whisper.

"You mean to tell me that I can buy your overpriced sewing needles and your stale crackers, but I can't sit here at this counter and rest my feet for five minutes before I walk home?"

"That's right," Jimmy says, pointing to a Whites Only sign above the coffee machine. His voice is hard, but I can detect a note of fear underneath.

"Well, I'm gonna sit here and rest my feet. You'll just have to go get the manager if you don't like it and carry me on out."

No, Sophie, I think. Jimmy disappears through a door behind the counter. *Just go on home, Sophie, and don't cause a commotion.* Sophie's feet have been aching something awful lately and it makes her ornery when she has to stand on them for any length of time. She sometimes can't take another step until she sits down to rest them. I just wish she happened to be in the park or in the kitchen when her feet acted up—not in Wallace's.

"She's a troublemaker," Katie whispers in my ear. "My mama says Sophie's gonna get herself thrown in jail one of these days for talking out like she does. Don't you just hate it when colored don't know their place? My mama would never keep a girl like Sophie. She's all trouble."

My face is red-hot. I can just hear Mrs. Blanchard talking about Sophie. Mrs. Blanchard refers to the women who work for her as girls, though most are old enough to be her mother. I once heard her say that Sophie had the sense of a dog. I wish Katie and her mother would restrain themselves from talking about Sophie getting thrown in jail. Like I haven't known this was a possibility all along.

Sophie sits at the counter, takes off her shoe and rubs her left foot. She says her feet are bad from carrying around too much weight for too many years.

Nigel Wallace, who is married to Jimmy's aunt Betty, comes up to the counter with Jimmy behind him. The customers at the lunch counter stop drinking their coffee and turn to watch.

"Oh, boy," Katie whispers. "Sophie's gonna get thrown out. Mister Wallace has no patience for sassy Negroes."

Mr. Wallace looks like what Jimmy will probably look like in thirty years—bald, with a little paunch where his flat stomach used to be. But I don't say this to Katie, who's beaming at Jimmy.

"Now, auntie," Mr. Wallace begins, his voice all sweet and sugary. "You know you can't sit at the counter. This is for the white folks."

Sophie looks right at him. *No, Sophie,* I think. *Don't say it. Please don't say it.*

"In the first place, I am not your auntie," Sophie says,

not budging from the stool. "And secondly, I'm not eating any of your white food. I'm resting my feet before I walk home."

"You know, I'm surprised that you're still alive, auntie, with all the trouble you cause." He says the word *auntie* louder than before. "You certainly do have yourself quite a mouth, and I can't have that in here. Maybe I better reconsider letting Negroes into my store from now on, if they're gonna make trouble. It's not good for business. Is it, boys?" Mr. Wallace says, winking at two gentlemen at the counter.

The two men stand up and walk behind Sophie. They're big, and when Mr. Wallace gives a nod of his head they put their arms under Sophie's armpits and with some effort heave her off the stool and drag her toward the door. Their faces strain under her weight and she's not helping them any. I feel a rush of anger. I want them to take their hands off Sophie.

"Don't be coming back, now, auntie, you hear?" Mr. Wallace yells after her. The two men drag Sophie to the door and push her roughly outside, brushing their hands off on their pants, like they just did a good day's work. Mr. Wallace and Jimmy laugh, as if it's a big joke watching Sophie trying to get her balance, dropping her bags on the sidewalk. I step out from behind the shelves and start moving toward the door. Sophie needs my help. I can't just stand here and watch them treat her like this. Like she's nothing.

"Where are you going, Celli?" Katie catches me by the arm. "Leave her be. She deserved it for giving Jimmy a hard time and talking back to Mr. Wallace."

"I have to help her, Katie," I say, pulling my arm out of her grasp.

"Not in front of Jimmy," she says, horrified. "I don't want him thinking we know her. Imagine how that would look. If you go to her then you can forget ever coming to the movies with me again."

"Katie, you don't understand!" My voice is loud and Mr. Wallace glances over at us.

"Now, just let her be," Katie whispers, smiling at Jimmy and Mr. Wallace and patting me on the arm. "You'll only get her into more trouble." I look at Katie, wondering what she could mean. How could I possibly get Sophie into more trouble than she gets into herself?

"She's used to it, Celli. All black folk are used to it. Look," she says, pointing at the window. "See, Sophie's all right. She's going home where she can't cause any more trouble."

Sophie stands up and gives one last glance in the store window as she limps slowly past. She looks directly at me, but I'm not sure if she can see me through the glare of sun on the glass. I feel my face turn hot with shame.

"Come on, Celli," Katie says, leading me to the soda fountain. "I'll buy you anything you want."

✦ ✦ ✦

Sabrina was almost two hours long and I had Sophie so heavy on my mind I can't even remember how it ended. I just wanted to get home and see if Sophie was all right. I was ashamed of myself for letting Katie talk me out of helping her. But with all those folks staring at me, I felt embarrassed to know her, and mad, too. Sophie knows the rules and yet she's always pushing on them, trying to nudge them out of the way so she can go about her life. It's like she won't accept things the way they are. I wish she would. I worry about Sophie. I do. I don't want to lose her.

Without a daddy our family feels kind of lopsided. Like a scale that's too light on one side, leaving the other end high up in the air, blowing in the breeze. Except when Sophie's around. She's like a lucky copper penny with enough weight to balance us out.

My head is pounding from worry and too many Sugar Babies. I need to walk in the fresh air and even though it's close to ninety degrees, it feels good to be outside.

"Let's go home by way of the trestle," I suggest.

"If you want," Katie says glumly. To her great anguish, Jimmy Lee Bottle showed up halfway through the first part of *Sabrina* with Beverly Mahoney. They sat two rows in front of us and Katie watched every move they made. Good thing they didn't kiss each other or Katie would have been beside herself.

"You know, Celli, I think Jimmy just feels sorry for Beverly Mahoney with that big nose of hers and all."

"Beverly doesn't have a big nose," I say. Katie turns to me as if I've betrayed her.

"It's crooked, Celli. You just don't notice things like I do. It's almost shaped like a hook. Like a witch's nose. Maybe she'll grow a big hairy wart on it one day."

"Stop it, Katie," I say. "Let's talk about something else."

"Yeah, who wants to talk about Beverly Big Nose anyway?" Katie says, sulking. But she can't think of anything else to talk about, so we walk in silence down Fern Street and cut through the patch of woods behind the Methodist church.

Sophie says that the town of Mystic was built in the middle of one of the biggest patches of kudzu anywhere in the world and the vine is always trying to take the town back. That's all there is behind the church. Vines come all the way up to the back door of the vestry and then stop, as if afraid to go any further for fear of eternal damnation. Kudzu is not particular about where it winds itself. It'll wrap around your ankles if you stand still in it too long and follow you in the house if you leave the door open, but somehow I think this vine has got enough sense to stop where it is.

There is a narrow footpath running through the vine and weeds. It branches into two paths early on. If you go right, it takes you to the Screaming River. No one goes that way that I know of, it's all overgrown. Folks say it's haunted by the ghosts of the swampers and if you happen to go down there in the evening, when their spirits are greedy, they might just eat you up for supper to quench their terrible hunger for human compassion. I have no intention of ever going down to the banks of the Screaming River in the day or night.

If you go left, it takes you to the railroad trestle. Katie and I take this path because it is a shortcut to my house. We descend a steep rocky bank to the edge of the tracks.

I can tell right away that we aren't the only ones down here. Voices echo from up on the trestle.

"Look, Celli," Katie says, pointing up into the trees. "Isn't that Ellery and Shelby?" I can make out the back of Ellery's frizzy hair and Shelby's bright red shirt, stretched around his body like a big cherry Life Saver. They're taking turns throwing stones off the trestle, trying to see who can hit the crossing sign right in the middle of the X.

"Let's spy," Katie whispers, the mischief back in her eyes.

We crouch down in the weeds and hide ourselves in the prickers, weave a little kudzu vine in our hair. There isn't much to see until Ellery and Shelby climb down off the trestle onto the tracks. They walk along the rails with their arms out to their sides, seeing who'll be the first to fall or twist his ankle. I know Ellery jumps freights and takes joyrides. If Mama or Sophie ever found out, they'd wring his neck. But I don't think that's what Ellery and Shelby are doing today.

Ellery pulls shiny pennies from his pants pocket. He trades for them at the Emery Bank. He collects old tarnished coins all week and slips them under the glass to Miss Ferguson, the bank teller, on Saturday mornings. She pushes back a whole pile of shiny new ones.

For twenty feet, they place pennies an inch apart, straight in a line. Then Shelby spits in the center of each one. Makes me wonder how any kid can have so much spit inside him. Shelby is plump and juicy from eating all his mama's shoofly pie, so he must have reserves. He plasters those pennies with a goober each, then they sit on the rails and wait for the 3:40 to reach the trestle. They stand right on the tracks, even though they can see the train coming straight for them and the ground is shaking. I look over at Katie and I'm not sure which one of us is gonna scream first. We both just freeze instead. The conductor pulls on his horn maybe five hundred feet away and Shelby jumps, then Ellery, into the bushes right below us and the train rolls over every one of those shiny pennies, turning them into big stretched-out disks of copper.

Ellery keeps hundreds of these melted disks in a cigar box under his bed. I've seen him take them out and wash them, dry them, put them back. Ellery's clearest memory of Daddy is going down to the rail station in Atlanta with him, watching the trains go by and placing pennies on the track. Daddy gave the cigar box to Ellery the night before he left.

I went into Ellery's room once when he wasn't around and opened up his box. I ran my fingers over the shiny copper circles. Most have some trace of Lincoln's face left, though the proportions are all wrong. The nose is long as a pipe and curved to one side, or his beard is pulled far away from his chin so he looks like he has a horn growing there. But on some there is no trace left at all. Just a smooth copper oval. Like a frame with no picture inside. No image. Disappeared. Just like Daddy.

Katie wants to come over for a glass of lemonade before she goes home. She's so downhearted about Jimmy that even though I'm tired of listening to her, I invite her in.

Sophie is in the kitchen cooking up a batch of ginger-bread. I can smell it as I walk in the door. I don't know what to say to her. I feel bad about watching those men throw her out of Wallace's.

"Lemonade, please, Sophie," Katie says, plopping down in the kitchen chair. Sophie gives Katie a sour look and I walk over to the refrigerator.

"We have cola and orange juice," I say. Katie looks at me. She's used to ordering around the women who work for her. If I ever tried to give Sophie an order like that, she'd go over me up and down about manners and re-specting my elders. She'd ask me if I have two healthy legs to walk to the refrigerator and two strong hands to pour my own glass of lemonade. But Sophie is strangely quiet.

"Let's go outside, Katie," I say, carrying two glasses of

orange juice out with us. I have a bad feeling that Sophie saw us in Wallace's today and she's angry with me.

Katie and I sit on the back porch step and sip our juice. It must be almost one hundred degrees by now and Katie has a little sunburn beginning on the bridge of her nose. I'm lucky. Mama says I have enough pigment in my skin so I'll probably never burn.

"How does she get away with that?" Katie asks.

"Who?" I ask.

"Sophie. I asked her for lemonade. I even said *please* and she just ignored me. Who does she think she is?"

"She's Sophie," I say.

"It's not right, Celli. Your mama spoils Sophie. That's bad news."

"What do you mean?" I ask.

"My mama said that her mama had a girl once that was sassy and her mama put up with it. And then one night while they slept, that girl took all the silver and a heap of cash from the sugar canister and set the barn on fire. Mama said they were lucky she didn't poison their food while she was at it."

"Sophie would never do anything like that, Katie."

"How do you know?" asked Katie. "Dark folk are different, Celli. They're not the same as us. As soon as your back is turned they'll take advantage. They will. My mama says the Negroes today are not much different than the savages that first came over here."

I'm not sure if I should laugh or hit Katie across the

face to bring her to her senses. I can hear Sophie rustling around in the kitchen. I lower my voice. "You better not let Sophie catch you saying things like that."

"It's the truth," Katie says.

"It is not, Katie." My voice comes out louder than I expect. I've been keeping my feelings in all day and now they're coming out. "Your mama just doesn't understand, Katie. She's ignorant."

"Celli Jenkins, after I just took you for a malt and a movie you have the nerve to call my mama ignorant?" Katie's whole face is turning the same color as the bridge of her nose.

"She says a lot, Katie, but she doesn't understand what she's saying. She's just repeating what her folks told her without giving it consideration of her own. If your mama could talk to Sophie and get to know her, she'd feel different. Sophie says understanding is what most folks are lacking and if you don't have that you're just led around by fear."

"I don't know what you're talking about, Celli," Katie says, backing away from me as if she's suddenly realized I have some infectious disease. "Sophie sure has put some strange ideas into your head. I'm leaving."

"Fine," I say. My voice sounds tired, my face is hot and my insides are all riled up. *That's fine,* I think. *I'd rather wait until Sunday and play jacks with Tilly than hang around with you.*

"I think I'll go over to Vale Austin's house for the rest of the afternoon. Her girl, Ella, always serves us mint tea and cookies out on the veranda. I'd ask you to come, Celli, but I don't think you're invited over there anymore, am I right?"

I nod my head. Mrs. Austin doesn't want me playing with Vale. She doesn't trust me since Sophie got involved with the Movement. She's afraid I'll fill Vale's head with strange ideas.

I turn and walk back up the porch steps. I push against the kitchen door, but it won't give. I look up and Sophie is standing behind the screen, smiling down at me.

⋆ 5 ⋆
Pearl

I've decided on a white cotton dress with a lace slip that pokes out underneath for my meeting with Grandma Pearl. This meeting is all I've thought about since the day the letter came two weeks ago. That and trying to keep the letter away from Ellery. I still believe I'm doing the best thing for all of us. Grandma Pearl might be horrified at Ellery's table manners and decide never to visit us again. I figure that I'm just saving us all a lot of heartache.

I pull my thick brown hair up into a bun at the back of my neck and shine up my patent leather shoes. I don't like lying and I hardly ever do it, but I told Sophie I was walking to Bobbie Stanton's birthday party over on First Street. It's true that it's Bobbie's birthday today, but I am no longer welcome at the Stantons' house either. Bobbie's mama, like Mrs. Austin, doesn't like the fact that Sophie is involved with the Movement.

Mystic is a small town and lately Sophie has a way of bringing up the words *civil rights* in the presence of other maids, which makes the white folks nervous. Bobbie says her mama doesn't want me coming over anymore. She thinks I spend too much time with Sophie and have funny ways because of it. I don't know why Mrs. Stanton would think such a thing, as I have barely spoken two words to her in all my life, but sometimes when folks get an idea in their head about you, it's hard for them to change it.

Bobbie and I used to play jump rope in my backyard and eat Mama's greasy fried chicken. She isn't allowed to come over anymore. Sometimes I see her in the five-and-dime and I give her a wink or squeeze her hand at the counter while she's buying a pound of caramels and she'll give a wink or squeeze back. That's as far as we dare to go. Mrs. Stanton is always hovering nearby like a hawk.

I know Sophie is gonna be involved with the Movement no matter what I say, but I don't understand why it has to affect me. Why can't she just do it quietly? It's hard enough trying to fit in in this town, having no daddy and all, without Sophie making matters worse. Sometimes I think Sophie will ruin my social life forever.

At eleven-thirty I head downstairs and grab a tissue to stuff into the pocket of my dress. The month of July makes my nose run. Actually my nose runs most every other day of the year as well. Sophie says it's because I have too much grief in my soul over Daddy and it's got to get out somehow, so it runs out my nose. Sophie has some strange notions, but this is about the strangest.

There isn't anyone in the kitchen, so I sneak out the back door and skip to the sidewalk, head for the Elgin. It's a bright, humid day. The chokecherry trees are dropping fat, juicy blossoms on the blacktop.

As I round the corner to Elm Street, I get a pain in my stomach, like someone just released a whole sack of butterflies in there and they're bumping against my insides, batting their wings trying to get out. I have rehearsed what I'll say to Pearl in front of the mirror in my bedroom every night for the past two weeks, but when I try to think of anything I've practiced, that pain just comes into my stomach again.

Mrs. Gerard from the bakery passes me with a bag full of cinnamon buns and for a minute I don't recognize her. All I see is white hair and a cane and my heart leaps. I think it must be Pearl. An awful fear comes over me just then until I see the heavy framed glasses on Mrs. Gerard's face.

"Why, morning, Celli. Don't you look pretty today. My, my, like a flower," she says.

"Thank you, ma'am," I say, and keep on walking until I reach the Elgin.

The Elgin Hotel was built over one hundred years ago. It has a front porch that wraps all the way around it. Pansies and geraniums fill all the flower boxes. It's a huge white building with a fat brick foundation that has always reminded me of an ocean liner.

I sit in one of the tall rocking chairs on the porch and watch every woman over the age of forty who walks by, wondering. Mr. Elgin comes out on the porch. He is the great-grandson of the Mr. Elgin who built the hotel. He is a short, fat man with a slightly nasal voice that sounds likes it's coming at you through a tunnel. I tell him I'm meeting a friend for lunch and he brings me out a glass of water, inquires about Mama. Mama told me that way back Mr. Elgin had a crush on her. He wanted to marry her, but she said no. Mama was young and she was imagining a life far away from Mystic at the time, so Mr. Elgin married someone else.

"How's your mama, Celli?"

"Fine," I say. "She's up in Atlanta until the end of the month visiting my aunt Etta."

"Your mama is a pretty woman. Letting her out on her own in a big place like Atlanta, why, she might just come home with a new daddy for you."

"I already have a daddy, Mister Elgin," I remind him. "I don't need another one." Sometimes my tongue is sharp on the matter of my daddy. It makes me mad how folks just figure I want a new daddy when I haven't properly met the old one yet.

Mr. Elgin nods his head and quietly walks back inside. It's a known fact in this town that Mama is widowed, as that is what she and Grandma Flo tell anyone who asks, and I have come to understand that being both widowed and pretty is not a good combination in some folks' mind. It seems among the wives in town that beautiful, available women are just about as welcome as a rabid dog running loose down Main Street. If any of them really knew Mama, they'd know there was nothing to worry about. She doesn't want any other man besides Daddy and even if she did she's not the kind to take one that's already spoken for.

I finish my water and put the empty glass beside me and glance at the clock tower over city hall. Popping up among the trees are the square white signs of the protesters. The clock says 12:10.

There's a tap on my shoulder. I turn around to the dark, handsome face of Fergus Freeman, who buses tables at the Elgin.

"Well, hi, Fergus."

"Afternoon, Miss Celli. How are you on this fine day?" Fergus's eyes sparkle. Sophie says Fergus has such a bright spirit inside of him it's hard for her to see anything else, but that's not true for everyone.

Fergus's mama was black. His daddy was Jewish. He's tall and thin with beautiful blue eyes and mahogany skin and he always wears a black baseball cap on his head, even when he's working.

Fergus's Mama, Fanny, was a maid for the Freemans, a wealthy family up in Chicago. The Freemans' oldest son,

Ned, took a liking to Fanny and after several months in their employment, Fanny was expecting Fergus. When the Freemans found out, they sent Fanny home to her own mama in Mystic to have the baby and shipped Ned off to a fancy college in Europe. Sophie said it wasn't easy having a child of mixed color in Mystic. Fanny gave Fergus his rightful last name, Freeman, though she never married his father. "Hard enough being of mixed blood and mixed faith without being illegitimate on top of it," Sophie says.

Folks eventually found out Fanny had no husband, but by then most of the black members of the community couldn't help but like Fergus, with his big wide grin and easy ways. In fact, now many of the older white women in town have taken a fancy to Fergus. He runs errands for them, washes their cars and listens to their troubles. He works for Mrs. Adler, the bank president's wife, who treats Fergus like a son, making jams and sweets for him to bring home. Fergus has a way of making you feel happy just by standing next to you. Sophie says it's because he was born bright as the sun and nothing anybody does or says will change that about him.

After Fanny died a few years ago, Sophie took Fergus to live with her until he turned twenty-one. Now he has his own little house next to Sophie's. She's like a mother to him. She takes him to every Wednesday night mass meeting at Screaming River Baptist.

That's where I first met Fergus. At church. Fergus

never seems to have a care in the world, but Sophie says the town is divided over him. There are some folks who love him for his sweet nature and some who would be glad to get rid of him because of his mixed color. It's the white men, mostly, that he has to stay clear of. They don't like anybody who is different. And Fergus sure is different.

"If Fergus ever makes a mistake in this town," Sophie says, "some folks will be on him like a pack of dogs on a jackrabbit."

"Miss Celli, there's a lady waiting for you and . . . Mister Ellery?" Fergus whispers.

I jump up. "It's just me, Fergus. Ellery isn't coming today." Fergus nods his head.

"She's out back on the veranda, Miss Celli."

I didn't know the Elgin had a veranda. I only thought it had an extra-large stoop jutting off the back. Fergus leads me through the dining room. It smells like baked chicken and coffee. I've only been inside once before, when Mama got a raise at the old folks' home and she brought Ellery and me here for a chicken dinner all done up in fancy raspberry sauce with potatoes on the side sliced so thin you could see through them.

The room is cool and dim. Some light trickles in. The coolness creeps up my arms and the skin rises to tiny bumps. The whole place feels delicious. I follow Fergus's white coat to the veranda. It isn't much of a veranda. Like I thought, it's more like a small porch with two tables set at angles to one another. I wonder why Grandma Pearl didn't choose a table in the cool, quiet dining room instead of out here in the direct sun. At the table farthest from me, a small woman sits with her back to us.

"Just the young lady is here, ma'am," Fergus says, pulling the chair out for me. "I'll be back with the menus."

I come around and sit, looking down the whole time, feeling shy. I take the burgundy-colored napkin from the table and spread it on my lap before I dare look across the table at the woman sitting there. It gives me a moment to settle. I hear her pull her seat in and I glance up.

"Hi, honey," she says.

I look at her. I look into her dark eyes and I forget to breathe. She doesn't look like me. She doesn't look like Ellery. She looks like Sophie, only in a lighter shade of black. I think maybe it's Pearl's maid sent in her place. But then I figure she wouldn't be calling me honey, she'd be calling me Miss.

She stretches her hand across the table and places it on my arm.

"Celli. I'm glad you came to meet me. Ellery couldn't come?"

I don't say anything. Just look at the contrast of skin. Chocolate over vanilla, like Sophie says whenever I hold her hand. "We're just chocolate and vanilla." Sophie made a song about it once, though right now the words have gone on without me. It's nice being chocolate and vanilla with Sophie, but it's not the same with Pearl. She's not supposed to be chocolate. If she's chocolate, then I'm no longer vanilla.

"I imagine you're surprised to see me." I nod my head and look down at my lap.

"I don't look much like your daddy, do I?"

I shake my head. "A little," I say. "Your eyes are the same."

"Do you remember your daddy's eyes?" Her voice flickers with excitement, like she can't remember them herself but she's sure glad someone else can.

"From a photograph."

"Well, honey, about the only thing your daddy got from me was my eyes. He takes after his own white daddy for all the rest except maybe his hair is a little on the nappy side."

There is a long silence. Daddy's hair. Ellery's hair. Mama praying mine is straight as a poker.

"Ellery couldn't come today," I say. "He's busy." Pearl nods.

"I'll catch up with him tomorrow. But I'm glad you came."

"Does my mama know about . . . you?" I blurt out. "About Daddy?"

"Yes, honey, she knows. It was something she and your daddy kept to themselves. He didn't want there to be any trouble. Nobody knew about your daddy's color except for your mama. Around here white and black don't marry, Celli. Why, they can't even so much as look at one another without there being a big old fuss. But when you're in love like your mama and daddy were, nothing could keep them apart."

Fergus comes over with the menus. They're not the dining room menus. I've seen those before. These are the menus from the bar. At the Elgin they only serve colored out back and from the bar, which is more than any other restaurant in town will do. I don't have any appetite. I excuse myself to the ladies' room, where I throw up in the toilet once and dry my mouth with a rough paper towel. I hardly ever get sick, only if I have to ride in the backseat when Sophie is driving. Sophie's driving can make me lose my lunch quicker than anything. But this is a different kind of sickness. Sickness from being scared, from having the world turned upside down.

I look at myself in the mirror. Look at my white cotton dress, my pale skin. I don't want to go back out there. How could she do such a thing to me? Why didn't she just stay in Ohio instead of coming down here to eat out on the back porch like she doesn't matter? Like I don't matter. Like neither of us is good enough. I look again in the mirror above the sink into my own blue eyes and I think it must be a joke. It has to be. A mistake. I'll close my eyes and count to ten and when I go back to the table there will be a lovely white lady waiting for me. I wash my face with the pink perfumed soap from the dispenser on the wall, blow my nose and go back to the porch. She's still there. She's still black. Pearl sits up higher in her seat, looking concerned.

"Now, honey, I didn't mean to upset you. I guess you weren't expecting me to . . . look the way I do. Your mama hasn't told you about your daddy's color?"

"No, ma'am," I say, shaking my head slowly.

"I know living down here it makes a big difference. It sure does. I lived in towns like this all my life. But it's not like that everywhere, at least not as bad. Why, where I live in Ohio, folks can go eat anywhere they please and they don't have to sit out back either." I nod my head.

"I know," I say. "Mama told me it's different up north."

"Well, that's part of the reason I've come to see you now, Celli. I came down here with a few folks from my church for the big rally on Saturday. We drove down in my car yesterday, a couple of days before everyone else, to get settled in and talk to the members of one of the churches in the area. The rest are coming down in buses tomorrow morning and then they'll continue on into Alabama. That's why folks have been standing outside your courthouse this week. They're getting ready for the rally, too. Have you seen them, Celli?"

"I have. I know all about it. Folks at Screaming River Baptist have been talking about it for months. Reverend Small and Sophie are helping to organize it."

"Sophie?" Pearl asks.

"Yes, ma'am. Sophie watches Ellery and me while Mama's away in Atlanta. Sophie's a good cook and has a tendency to speak her mind. She can't help it."

"I think I'd like to meet Sophie," Pearl says, smiling. For a minute the picture of Daddy flies through my mind. *You smile like my Daddy,* I want to say, but I don't. I've almost convinced myself in a tiny corner of my brain that Pearl is just a nice old black lady, a friend of Sophie's, who has been so kind as to take me out to lunch and talk a spell on this fine, hot summer afternoon. No more.

"So, your mama is away in Atlanta?" Pearl asks.

"Yes, ma'am. She won't be home for another two weeks."

"I guess she didn't get my letter, then."

"No, ma'am."

Pearl smiles. "It's nice to keep things to yourself sometimes. Isn't it, Celli?"

"Yes, ma'am," I say, blushing. We sit in silence for a moment.

I can't think of a word to say, so I don't say anything. It doesn't present a problem, though, because Pearl talks enough for both of us, which is a relief.

She tells me about her life in Cleveland, how she's been a dressmaker there for over twenty-five years and how except for her cat, Shoofly, there's just her in a big old house. As long as I can keep Pearl's true identity in the back of my mind and not think of her as my grandma, my appetite returns. We eat cucumber sandwiches and deviled eggs, lemonade and melon soup. When dessert comes, strawberries and cream cake, I'm stuffed, but Pearl helps me out.

"Now, Celli, you must think it's strange for me to come around after all these years, but I got so curious about you and Ellery I just couldn't wait. I don't know where your daddy is anymore and I don't have any family after my papa died last year."

Disappointment settles in my stomach. The cream cake starts feeling mighty heavy all of a sudden.

"When I found out a group from my church was coming down to make our voices heard, I thought *Now is the time.*"

"Folks coming all the way down from Ohio?"

"Yes, they are. All the way from Ohio. A lot of folks want things to change, Celli. They want equal rights."

"I know. Sophie talks about it all the time." My voice must sound lower than a snake in tall grass, as Sophie says, 'cause I'm still getting over the fact that Pearl doesn't know where Daddy is, and I'm not doing such a great job of keeping her identity in the back of my mind. It's creeping forward.

"Well, honey, I didn't come to talk to you about that. Tell me about yourself."

"I can't think of anything to tell you," I say. "I'm feeling kind of poorly all of a sudden. I think I need to go home now. . . . Pearl." She comes around and pulls out my chair for me.

"Will you be all right getting home, honey?"

"Yes, ma'am," I say. "I know my way. Thank you kindly for the lunch." Pearl gives a little smile.

"If you want to reach me, I'll be staying out at the Horn Motor Lodge on the county road. Here's my phone number there." She opens up her big black pocketbook and retrieves a rectangular piece of paper, slips it into my palm as I stand up.

"You need anything, honey?" she asks.

I think about this for a minute. I want to tell her I need everything. I need my mama and my daddy and a grandma who looks like me. But I just shake my head and walk on home.

✦ 6 ✦
Mass Meeting

Sophie's late. She went over to visit Halia Monroe, who broke her leg falling off a ladder last week trying to pick a few withered plums off the tree in her front yard. Sophie took her some cold soup, biscuits and a cherry pie two hours ago and she's not home yet.

I don't mind being left alone in the daytime, but when the sun starts to set, I like someone older around to fight off the shadows. A real lonely feeling comes over me right before supper. I've had this feeling as long as I can remember. Usually I can be distracted from it by other people. When Mama is gone, I have Sophie to talk to, but when Sophie is gone, I only have myself. Sometimes I just sit and feel it. A cold hollow ache, like my insides are empty as a cave. I mentioned it to Mama once and she said she knew that feeling well. She said she's had that cold feeling in her belly ever since Daddy left.

Somehow at this time of the day it feels like family should be coming together for the evening instead of pulling apart. It feels like there should be more folks around besides me and Ellery, who doesn't do much to help with that cold feeling. He's either in his room reading comic books or out in the garage taking his bike apart and putting it back together again.

Sophie left a pan of corn bread and a dish of pork rinds on the stove top so all we have to do is serve it up on Mama's flowered china dishes, but even that seems like difficult work when I get that lonely feeling inside me. When Ellery comes in the back door, I tell him he can take his plate to his room and read a book until bedtime. He gives me a look like "Who made you boss" before heading upstairs. Ellery hates having me tell him what to do and never listens, but Sophie has reminded me so many times to keep Ellery in line that the orders just slip off my tongue before I can stop myself. I take a plate of pork rinds and return to the window seat.

This time of year the wisteria has wrapped around the porch post outside the window and the fragrance drifts in, filling the room with sweetness. I miss Mama. We used to sit here in the window when I was little and read fairy tales out of a big old book Grandma Flo gave me for Christmas one year. I'd snuggle down under her arm and take in the sweet, comforting smell of her body. She'd tickle me and hold me tight. Whenever I sit here, I think about Mama and tonight I wish she wasn't so far from me. I believe she could hug away this cold empty feeling in a minute.

I take three bites of corn bread and put my plate on the wood floor. I walk over to the mirror on the wall and look at myself, trying to find something of Pearl in my face. I've been doing this ever since I came home from the Elgin this afternoon. Every time I pass this mirror or the mirror in the bathroom, I linger for a while, looking for something that isn't there. I look hard, but all I see is myself and a bit of Mama mixed in.

I was so excited for the past two weeks waiting to meet my grandma and now I can't even think about Pearl without feeling like I'll be sick to my stomach. She said she might be staying on for a while, but I hope she leaves soon. I don't want to run into her in town. I don't want anyone knowing we're related. It's bad enough Sophie has all but ruined my social life. If it gets out that my own grandma is black, I might just as well pack my bags and leave Mystic forever.

I settle myself in the window seat and stare out through the kudzu that's taking over the window frame. Through the green vines, I see the angels sitting up in the crab apple tree. It's late for them. In fact, I've never seen them at this time of the day. They're taking turns hooking their knees over the branches and hanging upside down. Their braids fall in long cascades that almost touch the ground. One angel tickles another's bare belly. They go around teasing each other and swinging from their knees. I kneel on the cushion and put my chin on the windowsill and laugh to myself until they fly away, taking some of my loneliness with them.

✦ ✦ ✦

"Celli, where are you?" Sophie calls from the kitchen. I hear the thump of her bags on the floor and the squeak of the faucet as she turns it on for a drink. I'm glad she's home.

"I'm in here, Sophie," I say, keeping my place in the window seat. I just got settled. I'll wait for her to come to me.

"What are you up to, honey?" Sophie says. She's been on her feet too long today. She limps into the room, lowers herself into a chair, pulls off her shoes and sighs.

"Not much," I say. "How's Halia?"

"Well, considering she's got her leg wrapped all the way up to her stomach practically and it's over a hundred degrees in that little house of hers, I'd say she's in pretty good spirits. I think she'll live as long as she don't try picking any more dead plums for dinner." I nod my head.

"You seem mighty quiet tonight, Celli."

"I'm just tired, Sophie. I think since you're home now, I might go and get ready for bed."

"Well, honey, I'm not home for long. There's a meeting at the church tonight, remember? Tomorrow's the big day. The man from up north, who has organized the Freedom Riders, is gonna speak. I wouldn't miss it for the world."

"Oh, Sophie, do you have to go? I don't feel like staying home alone tonight."

"Where's that brother of yours?"

"He's upstairs in his room. But you know as well as I do that being home with Ellery is just as good as being home by yourself. He's not much company." Sophie smiles.

"You feeling a little lonesome?"

"Yes, ma'am. Why don't you stay home and teach me how to bake a cherry pie? There's still a whole bowl of cherries left in the fridge."

"That sounds nice, Celli. But I promised I'd be there. I'm gonna be speaking tomorrow and the reverend and I are the ones that invited the Freedom Riders to Mystic, so I gotta be there." Sophie pauses. "I guess you *could* come with me. Just this once."

Even though I've been wanting to go to a mass meeting with Sophie ever since she first told us about them, I don't want to go tonight. Pearl might be there, and besides, I don't want to see all the folks in the congregation, especially Tilly and Rosa. I feel funny. Maybe it's just my imagination, but ever since I found out about Pearl, I think everyone else must know about her, too. Maybe everyone at Screaming River Baptist knows and thinks that I'm just like them now. But I don't want to be like them. I want to be me. Like I've always been.

"I don't know, Sophie. I'm kind of tired."

"Am I hearing you right, girl?" Sophie says, sitting up in her chair, staring at me. Her hair is sticking up on the sides of her head like it does in this kind of warm weather and her face is all shiny. "You've been wanting to come to a meeting with me, haven't you? What's the matter?" Sophie gets up and shuffles across the floor in her bare feet. She pulls the bangs up off my forehead and touches the inside of her wrist to my skin, checking for fever.

"Cool as a cucumber."

"I'm just tired, like I said. Why don't you ask Ellery?"

"Huh," Sophie says, looking me up and down. "You know that boy has about as much interest in going to a meeting as I have in sitting by the tracks waiting for trains to pass by."

She's right. Just getting Ellery to church on Sunday can be a chore. He couldn't care less about Sophie's Movement. He still thinks it has nothing to do with him. It's strange knowing about Pearl when Ellery has no idea. Normally I'd be glad to know something my big brother doesn't, but I wish I didn't know this secret. It seems like I've saved Ellery a lot of worry by not telling him about Pearl. I wish I could trade places with him now.

"I'd say you're more than just tired. You want to tell me what's going on?" I know by the way Sophie's eyes are boring into mine that's she not gonna leave me alone until I either tell her what's on my mind or go with her, and I don't want to tell Sophie anything.

"All right, I'll go," I say, pulling myself to my feet. "I guess I'm not that tired after all."

"Mmm-hmmm," Sophie says, keeping her eye on me as I walk into the kitchen and take my sweater off the hook.

Screaming River Baptist is packed with people. I've never seen this little church so full. There are folks lined up along the walls, fanning themselves with hymnals in the warm night air. The room smells heavy with the scent of gladiolus from a vase in front of the pulpit. I look around the room for any sign of Pearl, but there are so many bodies around me I have to do my best just to stay near Sophie. Maybe if I stand behind her wide hips, no one will be able to see me. I used to do that when I was little—stand in back of Sophie in the kitchen, like some kids stand behind trees. Sophie's body would completely hide mine from view and Mama could never find me. But Sophie isn't standing still long enough tonight to hide behind. She's buzzing around, catching up on the news.

I stand with my back against the wall, trying to disappear. Old Mr. Gates brushes by me, smiles and gives a wink. Maybe it's just an ordinary wink or maybe he thinks he knows something about me, it's hard to tell. After he passes, a seat opens up in the back row and I slide into it.

Reverend Small comes out to the pulpit and the congregation quiets down. He's dressed in his shiny black Sunday robes and looks mighty handsome. Something about the way he stands there all tall and proud sends shivers up my arms and for a moment I forget about Pearl.

"Good evening," he says in a deep voice that vibrates through my chest.

"Evening, Reverend," folks reply, settling themselves in chairs or along the wall.

Reverend Small introduces a young white man named Manny O'Brien, who is here to tell us all about the Freedom Riders who are coming into Mystic tomorrow morning.

When Sophie first told me about the Freedom Riders, all I could picture was a bunch of folks coming into town on horseback, like in the Wild West, bringing law and order. Sophie says that's the general idea, only they'll be coming down in buses. Black and white folks sitting together. Black people not just in the back of the bus, but anywhere they like.

I overheard Grandma Flo tell Mama once that when the Negroes stop sitting in the back of the bus and start eating at the lunch counters, then that will be the end of the South as we know it. Unlike Sophie, Grandma Flo didn't seemed pleased about this fact. She was mighty upset.

Manny O'Brien clears his throat. He is tall and skinny.

He has freckles all over his pale face and his hair is the color of a carrot.

"We'd like to thank all you kind folks at Screaming River for inviting us here and standing with us tomorrow as we gather in front of the courthouse to make our voices heard. We'd especially like to acknowledge the hard work of Reverend Small and Sophie Carter." There is a murmur of voices from the front row and Bertha pats Sophie on the back.

"Mystic is the second town we've stopped at on our journey and we're hoping things will be peaceful here, but I want to tell you that they might not be." He glances over at Reverend Small. "As the reverend knows, I've come ahead with a few of my fellow organizers to prepare for the buses as best I can. Though Mystic is small, the opposition may be strong. We want to remind you all of the example of nonviolent protest given to us by Dr. Martin Luther King. Riders will disembark from the buses at the station on Elm Street. We will meet them there and walk over to the courthouse together, carrying signs. A few folks will speak. Beyond that, our demonstration will be silent."

If Sophie were sitting beside me at this moment, I'd elbow her in the ribs. But Sophie is sitting in the front row, whispering back and forth to the folks on either side of her. I don't think a silent protest is possible for Sophie.

I get shivers up my arms just thinking about what

these folks are planning for tomorrow. This rally is a dangerous idea and a waste of time. Why can't everyone just go on home and forget about it? I have a bad feeling in my stomach about the whole thing. But it's really none of my business. Sitting here watching and listening, I've decided that it's not my battle. Just because Pearl may be my grandmother doesn't mean I have to be part of this. There is no need for me to get involved with any Freedom Riders. Sophie can go off and get herself in trouble if she wants to, but I don't have to stand around and watch. My skin is white and that's all that matters in Mystic. I can just go on living like I've always done and no one will ever find out about Daddy.

Manny O'Brien sits down, the choir starts singing and Reverend Small calls the congregation up to the front of the church to pass out purple ribbons to everyone. He explains that we're supposed to wear them tomorrow as a symbol of our unity and as a reminder that God will be with us. All the folks in the row in front of me go up to the front of the church and come back pinning ribbons to their collar or the front of their dress. I don't go up, but Bertha has an extra. She turns and places a tiny ribbon in the palm of my hand. I quickly put it in the pocket of my sweater. It's a pretty little ribbon, but I won't be wearing it tomorrow, because I'm not gonna be there.

∗ 7 ∗
The Rally

Saturday morning. The day of chores, and fried croakers for breakfast. Sophie cooks the fish in a thick layer of grease in the frying pan and then dumps them onto a platter lined with paper towels to soak up as much excess as possible. Ellery likes them heavy with grease and so do I. Some Saturdays Ellery takes all the paper towels out of the kitchen and hides them in his bedroom so Sophie can't mess with the croakers.

"Listen here, you two," Sophie says, flipping the little fish onto our plates. "I'm gonna be gone to the rally all day today."

"Yes, ma'am," I say, pushing a fillet around with my fork, trying to ignore any mention of the day's events.

Ellery smiles. Saturday is his day to exchange pennies

and go down to the railroad tracks with Shelby. I can tell he's thinking about getting out of his chores for the whole day. He knows Sophie is preoccupied, and Sophie is hardly ever preoccupied.

"I got to go soon or I'll be late. I'm meeting the reverend and Audry Huckle at the bus station in fifteen minutes."

Sophie's all worked up this morning. She didn't even make orange juice or biscuits and she's moving fast. Sophie doesn't have the kind of muscles to move fast, but she's scurrying around the kitchen like she's got a wasp up her skirt. She can't find the purple ribbon Reverend Small gave her at the meeting last night.

"Lord have mercy, Celli, where did I put that ribbon?" Sophie rummages around in her purse. "I don't have time to look for it now."

I walk over to my sweater hanging on the hook by the back door and take the purple ribbon from the pocket.

"Here, Sophie, you can have mine," I say, handing it to her.

"Why, thank you, honey," she says, giving me a hug. "You sure you don't want to wear it yourself?"

"No, I'm sure, Sophie. You take it. I don't need it."

"Now, honey, if you feel strongly you want to come along, I won't stop you, but it might not be the place for you today. There's gonna be police. They might even take us to jail." Sophie has a strange look in her eyes, as if the idea pleases her. I feel a cold lump in my throat.

"Why do you have to go, Sophie? Why do you always have to go looking for trouble?"

"I'm not looking for trouble, honey. The white folks started the trouble a long time ago. I'm just trying to help set things right. Besides, I have to go. I'm gonna be standing up in front of the courthouse today speaking for my people."

"I don't want you to go to jail, Sophie," I say, folding my arms across my chest. "They feed you real bad food there and you never get to see the light of day."

"You got to believe, girl. You got to have faith. Don't go forgetting what the reverend said. Even if I go to the jailhouse, I won't be alone. I'll have my people with me and I'll have the Lord Jesus sitting right next to me in the dark eating cold, greasy croakers. Maybe He'll even bring some angels with Him and we'll all have us a party and make such a fuss they'll have to let us go."

I raise my head at the word *angels,* but Sophie isn't talking about my angels. I know Sophie isn't afraid of anything when she's got the Lord on her mind, but Mystic isn't like other places. If you're black in Mystic, you have to stay clear of trouble.

"If I'm not back by supper, heat up the beans and eat the rest of the sweet potato pie. Make Ellery wash his hands."

I look over at Ellery, who is standing next to the door waiting for Sophie to leave. Ellery is three years older than I am, but Sophie always puts me in charge of him if she goes out.

"Be your brother's keeper today, Celli," she says, wrapping up a stack of croakers in wax paper.

"I don't want to be his keeper," I say. "I'm only eleven years old. I don't want to be anybody's keeper. I don't want to make Ellery wash his hands. I don't want to make him do anything. He doesn't listen to me anyway."

"Yeah," agrees Ellery. "I'm the one who should be telling Celli what to do."

I stick my tongue out at Ellery and he tries to swipe me with his hand.

"Will you listen to yourselves," Sophie says, her voice suddenly hot and irritated. "Do you know what's happening in this town today? I'm fighting for my freedom and you're bickering like you've been doing ever since school let out. I'm gonna stand up for something important today and you're gonna stay out of trouble, do you hear me?" Sophie doesn't wait for an answer. She pushes through the door with her bag of croakers swinging behind her. "I'm late," she mutters under her breath, and walks down the porch steps, heading for the sidewalk. Her good Sunday shoes click out a beat on the hard cement as she turns onto Mariposa Drive.

Ellery and I look at each other like we always do after Sophie is through yelling. Like a storm has passed over and taken all the wind right out of us. Ellery shrugs and heads out the door right behind Sophie, walking quickly in the opposite direction.

I know where he's going. To the bank and then down

to the tracks to meet Shelby. I wait until Sophie is out of sight, then I slip on my loafers and follow her, keeping a good safe distance between us. I don't have to be part of this, but I can watch from the shadows.

I believe in angels and for Sophie's sake I even believe in Jesus some of the time, but with Mama and Grandma Flo gone, Sophie's all I have in the way of relations and I'm not going to let her go off by herself.

⋆ 8 ⋆
Freedom Riders

It's only nine o'clock, but already there's a crowd gathering on the lawn outside the courthouse. Waves of heat rise off the pavement, making the crowd look all shaky, like a mirage. I decided to wait here for Sophie and the Freedom Riders, 'cause there are more trees by the courthouse and it's easier to stay out of sight than at the bus station. I climb to the top of the courthouse steps and settle myself on a ledge jutting out from one of the pillars, where I can't be seen. The cool marble on my legs makes the heat bearable. It's going to be hotter when everyone gets here, and there isn't any shade left down on the grass. The old folks already took the good spots.

I hear singing and look down State Street. It's beginning. A large crowd of people with signs are moving in this direction. A police car follows closely behind. When they reach the courthouse steps, they fan out into a circle and Reverend Small makes his way through the crowd up onto the top step.

From behind the column I scan the crowd for Sophie, but she's only a dark head in a sea of mostly dark heads. I catch the words that float up to where I am. *Freedom. Integration. Nonviolence.* The reverend's voice is loud and today I must admit that is an advantage, considering the distance it has to carry through this crowd. The reverend reads a passage from the Bible about Moses leading the Israelites out of Egypt into the desert. He looks a bit like the picture of Martin Luther King Sophie has pasted up by the washing machine.

Two police officers get out of the patrol car and walk a little closer to listen. It's an advantage to be up above the crowd instead of inside it, because I can see what's happening. The reverend steps down and Sophie gets pushed up to the platform.

She clears her throat and looks out at the crowd. "Most folks around here know me," she begins. My heart is thumping. I can't believe the reverend is really going to let her speak. What if she says the wrong thing? What if she starts going on like she does and gets into trouble? But there's nothing I can do to stop her, so I sit real still so as not to miss her words getting carried away on the breeze.

"I been known to speak my mind on occasion." A roll of laughter rises up, then settles down. "Well, I guess I finally got a place to put my mouth to good use today. Thank you, Jesus, for bringing all these folks together. I know things are gonna change. I can feel it in my bones. This is our time to stand up. I say we got to stand up!" The crowd cheers.

From the direction of Elm Street another crowd appears and my stomach lurches. I can see them coming, but no one else can. I recognize Mr. Wallace and Mr. Bottle walking in the lead, and from the way they're walking, I know they mean business. Sophie and I are the only ones whose backs are not turned, but Sophie is so busy talking she doesn't notice them. When Mr. Wallace and the others reach the sidewalk, they surround the protesters and start chanting "Yankees go home" and the freedom marchers turn around to face them.

One teenage boy stands up on the bronze statue of the Lost Soldier of Mystic. A memorial to all the men who never found their way back home after the First World War. The boy hangs his arm around the soldier's waist.

"Why don't you sit down, old lady?" he yells. It's Henry Spigget's oldest boy. Sophie used to work for the Spiggets, ironing sheets. She said they had a mean streak, every last one of them. Said that, like a lot of men in Mystic, they were so full of hatred toward black folks they'd start a fight over the smallest thing.

The marchers are silent. The air feels thick and heavy. My heart is pounding. I can tell Sophie is trying hard to hold her tongue.

"Why don't all you Yankees go back where you come from? We don't need no more nigger-Jews coming down here and destroying private property. Ain't nothing gonna change in Mystic." I don't know what he's talking about—the marchers haven't destroyed anything—but whatever it is, it's got him all riled and the other men with him look ready for a fight.

A white freedom marcher puts down his sign slowly and goes over to Laud Spigget, that's the boy's name. "We're having a peaceful demonstration here today, son. Why don't you let this lady finish her speech now? We don't want any trouble."

"She ain't no lady. She's just a dumb nigger."

A silence sweeps through the crowd. There's a feeling in the air like right before a storm hits. Still, but full. Heads turn and I spot Pearl standing up against the trunk of an elm tree, waiting with everyone else for Sophie's reaction. Sophie just stands tall, staring down at the Spigget boy impatiently, like she's got more important things to do right now than respond to his name-calling. He stares back and it seems for a minute he's gonna call her that word again.

I hate that word. I hate the way folks say it. Even the black folks. Like it's the filthiest, dirtiest thing. Like something thrown away to rot in the sun. Makes my stomach turn when I hear it. Makes me want to jump in the river and wipe off all the grime of the word that's settled on my skin.

The Spigget boy says something I can't hear before lunging forward and shoving the white man in front of him to the ground. The silence breaks—it feels like something exploded. Things happen fast. There's more shoving. Someone starts throwing rocks. People scream. The police push their way into the group and the whole crowd moves into the street like a giant wave. I feel like I'm in a bad dream. I step out from behind the column and just watch it all. Sophie looks up and spots me. She looks at me real hard, then gives a smile. Next thing I know a rock hits Sophie alongside her head and she falls.

"No!" I scream. But no one can hear me. Folks gather around Sophie and I can no longer see her. I run down to the crowd, but they're taking her away. People push and shove all around me. It's like being trapped inside the fun house at the fair, where everywhere you turn there are mirrors and no way out. I'm afraid I'm gonna get hit by one of the police, who are swinging their sticks in all directions. But I don't even care. I've got to get to Sophie.

A black man appears beside me, takes me by the hand and leads me under a magnolia tree.

"Honey, you get on home as fast as you can. This is no place for you today."

"But Sophie! I have to help Sophie." Just then a police wagon pulls up and the officers start piling people in the back. Sophie and the reverend are among them, but I don't see Pearl. Someone grabs the black man by the arm and pulls him away from me toward the wagon.

My knees are shaking and I think I'm gonna pass out, but if I sit down now, I'll be trampled. I'm smaller than everyone else, so I dodge and weave my way through the crowd until I reach the sidewalk, then I take off running.

There are police cars blocking State Street, so I go the back way over to Main. I take the alley between Henley's Super Duper and the dry cleaner's. The air in the alley is heavy with rotten cabbage and cleaning fluid and, from somewhere farther off, the smell of burning rubber. My heart is beating fast and I stop to catch my breath.

In the shadows ahead of me, I see a figure, frozen, crouched behind a garbage can. Blue eyes stare out at me. It's Fergus! I'm so relieved to see someone I know I start to say "Hi, Fergus," but I stop myself 'cause he has his index finger up to his lips for silence and his eyes are filled with fear. I just stare at him for a while until he gestures with his hand for me to move on along. Even though I want to ask him what he's doing there, I obey. He looks so serious I don't dare refuse.

Coming out of the dark coolness of the alley, I shield my eyes from the bright light. The smell of burning rubber is stronger out in the street. From over near the bus station, a cloud of black smoke rises up over the trees and moves in my direction. I can just make out the back end of a Southern Transit bus all blackened by smoke.

People on the street are running every which way. A fire truck speeds past me, siren blaring. I cover my ears. It feels like the whole world is spinning out of control. *This must be what a war looks like,* I think. *Maybe this is a war.*

I'm scared to the bone and thirsty from the smoke and heat. I don't think I can make it home without stopping for water. I head down the street toward Wallace's, but there's an even bigger crowd outside the five-and-dime. People are yelling and the front window is all gone, just shards of glass lying all over the sidewalk.

"We got to find that Jew-boy," I hear a man yell.

I duck underneath the shade of the awning over Arrow Shoes near the entrance of the alley and watch. I've never seen anything like it. Mr. Garris from the garage and George Downey from the savings and loan are shouting and swearing, their faces hard and mean. They're saying hateful things.

They're looking for Fergus. I know they are. Sophie was right when she said there are some folks in this town who would be after Fergus in a flash as soon as anything bad happens. All he has to do is be in the wrong place at the right time and they'll get a scent on him and track him down like a dog.

✦ 9 ✦
The Ribbon

The whistle on the firehouse blows twelve noon. I've been waiting at the entrance of the alley for the crowd to break up, too afraid to move. I've just been standing here thinking about what Sophie says about faith. How when you're in need you got to do two things. You got to ask for help and then believe help will come. I've been asking the Lord to send down rain to cool off these folks' heads and bring them back to their senses. But I guess the Lord has something else in mind. It's not raining, but it's got to be over 110 degrees in the shade and no one, no matter how mad they are, can stand out in the direct sun on concrete for very long without having to go cool off somewhere. After a while most of the folks start heading for shade. Only one group of boys lingers on the curb by the five-and-dime, but I'm so thirsty and tired I have to pass them and get on home.

"Hey, little girl," one of the boys yells.

I look behind me to see who he's talking to. I am the only one on the sidewalk now. My heart starts racing.

"I saw you over at the courthouse with all them darkies. You probably know where that Jew-boy is hiding out."

My legs are shaking. The boy who's talking is Hank Spigget, Laud's younger brother.

"Hey, you don't have to be afraid of us, honey," Hank says, pulling the white hood of his sweatshirt up and grinning at me. I bet he has his own Klan hood at home, hung next to his daddy's. He tosses a rock from one hand to the other. "Too bad about that window breaking, isn't it?" He looks over at his buddies and laughs. "I'd hate to see anything like that happen again, wouldn't you? I guess when you let those people sit wherever they like, all kinds of things can happen." I look into his cold gray eyes and I don't say a word. He walks close to me, so close I can feel his hot breath on my neck as he speaks. "Maybe we'll pay you a visit one night, little girl."

I remember what Sophie told me about never showing fear to any animal 'cause they can smell it. She was talking about dogs at the time, but I think it'll work in this situation, too. I can't speak. If I speak, I'll cry. I tilt my head up and start walking, pushing my fear way down into my belly, where no animal could get a scent of it.

I turn the corner, cover my ears and run the rest of the way home.

✦　✦　✦

The first thing I do when I push open the kitchen door is splash my face with water from the sink. Then I cut a piece of Sophie's rhubarb pie, which is sitting out on the counter. I want to taste something she's made, something her hands have touched, to remind me that just a few hours ago everything was normal. But my stomach is too jumpy to eat anything just yet, so I sit down on a chair with the pie in front of me and stare into space. My heart is beating like a rabbit's, but other than that I feel nothing. Numb.

Only one thought comes to mind. I want to talk to Mama. She calls every Sunday night while she's away, but I need to hear her voice now. When my legs feel solid enough to stand on, I get up and rummage through the kitchen drawers until I find the small directory Sophie sometimes wedges into the side of one of the drawers so it won't fall out. I look up Etta Holbrook in the Atlanta phone book and dial the number.

"Please, Mama," I whisper. *"Please answer."* The phone rings and rings. Finally someone picks up. "Hello?" I say. "Mama?"

"No, this is Etta," the voice answers.

"Aunt Etta? This is Celli. I was just wondering if my mama is around. I'd like to speak to her." I actually want more than just to speak to her. I want to wrap my arms around her neck and never let her out of my sight again. What does she mean by leaving me in such a mess? I'm only eleven years old and I'm put in charge of Ellery, who is probably standing in the middle of the train tracks this minute waiting for the 1:45 to pass through, and Sophie's in jail and maybe dead, the whole town is after Fergus Freeman, and I have a grandma I didn't even know I had who's the color of coffee. "Come home, Mama," I want to say. "Everything is such a mess. Get on home and help me." But I don't say any of these things, because Mama isn't there. Aunt Etta says she'll leave her a message, but Mama has gone off on a picnic with some friends. She'll be home later. I thank Etta and hang up. I'm just thinking about calling Grandma Flo at Gerty's house when I catch sight of the angels in the backyard, dancing around the cherry tree.

As soon as I sit myself down on the back step to watch, they stop dancing and look at me. They have never done such a thing. Since they first began visiting, I've wanted nothing more than for them to look at me, but now it feels like too much. I'm not sure what to do. Should I meet their eyes or look above their heads? The harder I try to avoid their gaze, the more I find myself looking directly into their eyes. One angel has brown eyes. The other two have green. For a moment I think they might speak to me. They might just walk over like any girl my age and say "Hey, Celli, how ya doing?" Instead, the smallest angel bends over and picks something up from the grass and walks over to me, holding out her hand. Sophie's ribbon.

The angel places the deep purple ribbon in the center of my palm and it feels like a cool breeze passing over my skin. Then she smiles and lifts off. The other two angels follow her. I watch them as they hover above the huckleberry bushes and disappear over the trees.

I sit on the back step for a long time, pulling the ribbon through my fingers, feeling a little dazed. I sit there until the light begins to change and the shadow of the willow tree dances against the side of the house. I don't know what to think of this gift. What am I supposed to do with it?

"Miss Celli." I turn my head.

"Miss Celli," the voice whispers again.

In the shadow of the garage I can see a hunched figure walking slowly around our old lawn mower and then across the yard to the back porch. It looks like an old lady. Housecoat, straw hat and a pair of buckled-up shoes. I can't place her in my mind, though there is something familiar about her long stride. The woman makes her way along the side of the porch and crouches down next to me. She tips back her hat, revealing a pair of sparkling blue eyes.

"Fergus!"

I'm too startled to move. It has been a strange day. I didn't think it could get any stranger.

"Miss Celli. I sure am glad to see you." Fergus's face is all sweaty and he smells faintly of rotten cabbage. Chester must have caught the scent, too, because he wanders over for a sniff. Fergus freezes up and I realize he's probably been avoiding dogs all afternoon.

"Don't worry. It's just Chester. He won't bark if you let him smell you." Fergus stands stiffly while Chester sniffs around. Satisfied, the dog lumbers off to lie down under the peach tree.

"Fergus, how did you get here? Folks are looking all over for you."

"Only by the grace of God did I make it," he says, looking over his shoulder. "The crowd broke up at Wallace's. I heard someone say they were going to check the alleys, so I had to move. I crawled through the basement of the dry cleaner's shop. That's where I found these clothes." He gives the dress a little swish around his knees and we both laugh with relief.

"While I was in that dark basement, Miss Celli, a thought come to me. Something my mama told me once. She said that sometimes when folks get an idea in their heads, they can't see nothing else even if it's right under their nose. I figured if all those folks were looking for Fergus Freeman, a skinny black man running for his life, they weren't going to bother a poor old lady walking home from the market. So I grabbed up this old shopping bag," he says, placing a wrinkled canvas bag at my feet. "And I stuffed some rags in here," he says, plumping up his bosoms. "Then I walked down Elm Street real slow, right past the courthouse, and no one even looked at me twice."

"You sure are brave, Fergus," I say, looking down at his bosom, "but you got a terrible sense of fashion." Fergus laughs and I can see the gap between his front teeth.

"Did you break that window, Fergus?"

"Of course not. Why would I do something like that? A couple of the Freedom Riders tried to sit down at Wallace's lunch counter and folks got mad. Someone threw a rock and it hit the window. I was coming out of the Humdinger when it happened and one of them Spigget boys started in on me, so I took off."

Fergus is silent for a moment and a picture of Hank Spigget with a rock in his hand flashes through my mind. Fergus lowers his head and shakes it slowly back and forth. When he speaks again, his voice is more urgent. "I didn't do it, but the white folks think I did and they got the say, don't they? I got to get out of town, Miss Celli. Is Sophie around?"

"No, Fergus, Sophie's in jail." My throat catches and my eyes start to fill up. Something about hearing the words come out of my mouth makes the whole thing real.

Fergus's shoulders slump. I can tell he was counting on Sophie to tell him what to do next.

"Now, Miss Celli, it'll be all right," Fergus says, putting his arm around my shoulder. "Sophie is strong. She'll be fine. You know what the reverend says, we got to have faith now more than ever." I look up into Fergus's beautiful blue eyes and I wonder how anyone in his particularly bad situation could believe such a thing.

"What do you have there?" Fergus says, trying to distract me from my worries. I've been wringing the ribbon around my fingers so many times it's gone all curly.

"This is Sophie's ribbon. The ang—I mean . . . I . . . found it in the grass," I say, wiping my eyes.

Fergus reaches into his pocket and pulls out an identical ribbon and a smile comes over his face. A big radiant smile.

"I know what we got to do, Miss Celli."

The bicycle was Fergus's idea. I wanted to drive the Dart, but Fergus talked me out of it.

"Someone is gonna see you on the main road, Miss Celli. They know that's the car Sophie drives and she's in jail. You'll be stopped for sure. Besides, you're too young."

"Well, how else am I gonna get somewhere fast if I can't drive the car?" I ask Fergus, still uncertain that I'm even going to follow through with his plan.

Fergus's eyes wander past me. "I spotted something when I was hiding in here," he says, opening the door to the garage.

As soon as I turn on the light, we both see it. Fergus pulls off the sheet. Ellery's bike. All red and shiny, parked in the center of the garage on a layer of newspapers. He must be close to taking it out on the road.

I shake my head. "No, Fergus. Ellery might be home any minute. He'd kill me. It's the Bowden Space Lander." I'm surprised to find that it actually looks a lot like the one in Nickel's window. "He's been working on this bike since school let out, Fergus. He won't let me touch it. He doesn't even want me in the same room with it. He's planning to take it to the Macon Carnival at the end of the summer. It's the only thing he cares about." But Fergus isn't listening. He walks around to the front of the bike, switches on the headlamp and smiles.

✵ 10 ✵
Celli's Ride

Fergus's plan is for me to ride Ellery's Space Lander to the Screaming River Church after nightfall to ask for help. Nightfall is almost six hours away, but Fergus doesn't think it's safe for me to go now. So we wait. He is convinced that the congregation will meet there this evening once the confusion of the day dies down and people start thinking about what to do next. I'm not so sure, though, because the reverend is in jail.

Both of us are too nervous to concentrate on much of anything. Fergus studies road maps spread out on the kitchen table. He traces his fingers along the blue lines of highways heading north as we try to carry on simple conversations about folks we know from church. But I know what we're both thinking the whole time—the sooner the sun sets, the better.

After hours of waiting, the light finally begins to fade and Fergus starts packing me a paper bag with a bottle of water and two apples inside. He says if I go the back way, it'll take me less than half an hour, but it could take longer if there are folks around. By *folks* Fergus means white folks looking for him.

"Stop once and have the water and an apple, Miss Celli. It'll give you energy." I nod my head.

"You sure you know the roads well enough now?" Fergus asks. I nod my head again. We've gone over the route a hundred times. I know it by heart.

Fergus leaves his dress on in case anyone gets the idea that he's at our house, which they might, knowing he's a friend of Sophie's. He'll hide in the cellar as soon as I leave and not come out until I give three knocks on the cellar door when I return. If I return. I can't even think about what I'm planning to do tonight. When I do, my throat starts to close up and I feel like I can't breathe.

"I don't know if I'm the right person to do this, Fergus. What if someone stops me and asks me what I'm doing?"

"Where's Ellery?" Fergus asks.

"I don't know. He should have been home hours ago."

"Well, if anyone stops you, you just tell them you're out looking for your brother."

"What if that doesn't satisfy them? What if they don't

leave me alone?" I'm thinking about the boys outside the five-and-dime. I'm thinking about the Klan.

Fergus ties his purple ribbon together with Sophie's and places it in my hand. He reaches under his dress and pulls out his black cap from the back pocket of his pants and fits it on my head.

"I don't know much, Miss Celli, but I do know this. There are two things in life. There's fear and there's love and what you're doing tonight is for love. You just ride toward the light of Reverend Small's church and you'll know this for yourself."

I can't bring myself to say to Fergus the words that I truly feel. I don't believe anyone will be there. With the reverend in jail, I bet the whole congregation is hiding out like Fergus is, and I don't have the kind of faith he's talking about. Sophie has it, but I don't think it's inside of me.

Fergus looks me deep in the eye. "You're my angel tonight, Miss Celli."

I wish he hadn't said that. I could have found a hundred good reasons not to go if he hadn't. But he said exactly what Sophie would have said if she were here. He puts his hand on my shoulder and then disappears into the cellar and I give my shoelaces an extra knot.

I walk out into the night in my dark clothes and strap the bag to the back of Ellery's bike. The crickets are loud tonight, for which I am glad. I'm hoping they'll cover up the sound of bike tires on gravel.

The night is clear and a warm breeze blows the smell of wisteria into my nose. There is something about the smell of wisteria on a warm night in summer that fills me with hope—which is exactly what I need.

I pull Fergus's cap down low and climb up onto the seat. The Space Lander is a little big for me. I hope I don't wreck it. Ellery would never forgive me. I start pedaling. If I don't leave now, I'll never go. I head down Mariposa and over to Spring Street, avoiding the Halversons' big house on Maple Avenue. I've heard that Mr. Halverson and his sons are big in the Klan. They're probably out looking for Fergus right now.

I hear a dog bark somewhere in the distance and I pedal faster. There are a few streetlights that guide me down Liberty Street and then it's black again. I feel safer in the darkness because there is less chance of someone seeing me, but when I look ahead and there is nothing but night, fear starts to fill my stomach. There is a glow of light from the town behind me, so I don't need to turn on the headlamp just yet. I'll save the batteries for Sophie's Road, which is lined on both sides with willow trees. I imagine at this time of night it can get pretty dark out there.

I pedal through the east side of town and then when the pavement gets rough and gradually turns to dirt, I know I'm on the west side. Every muscle in my body relaxes. There is no one on this side of town who would hurt me. I've never thought of it like that before, but it's true. On the east side there are plenty of folks ready to do you harm if you think different than they do, but not here. It strikes me funny all of a sudden that Katie Blanchard is afraid of walking down Sophie's Road at night 'cause she thinks she'll turn black and I can hardly wait to get there.

I'm so tied up in my own thoughts I almost don't stop quick enough to avoid the lights. A car is coming down the road. I jump off Ellery's bike and push it into the trees and wait for the car to pass. It seems like forever before it reaches me, moving slow. There's a white man driving and another one hanging out the window.

"I swear I seen something move up here, Burt." I don't dare breathe. If they spot me, they'll take me back to town and maybe to jail and then who'll help Sophie and Fergus.

The man hanging out the window starts shining a flashlight around the woods. Maybe if I were on foot, I could go undetected, but with Ellery's shiny bike they'll see me in a minute.

I do something I have never done on my own before. I start praying. Silently, of course. *Dear Lord, please help me. I know in the past I haven't had much faith, but I need some tonight. I'm the only one who can go to the church. Use me as your instrument.* I've heard Sophie say this same thing before, and it sounds good now, anything sounds good. I place my hand over Sophie's and Fergus's purple ribbons in my pocket. *I believe you can help me, God. Thank you for showing these men home to their beds for the night.*

"Damn it, Burt." The man hanging out the car window pulls inside and fiddles around with the flashlight.

"Dead, Burt, the damn thing is dead." It must be Burt Halverson and one of his buddies. I don't hear anything else, because the man rolls up the window and the car speeds up and heads down the road toward town, sending a cloud of dust behind it. I whisper a thank you to God under my breath. Maybe praying does do something after all.

I guess I was wrong to think I was safe here. Of course, anyone looking for Fergus is gonna be searching out this way tonight. I'll have to take a different route.

I don't want to, because there's only one other way. But no one else will be down there, the path is too rough. I would give anything for another alternative. In fact, I'm just about to turn back around and head for home when I remember Fergus's words. *There's fear and there's love.*

I wish I could just let everyone take care of themselves tonight. Go home to bed where I'd be safe. But somehow Fergus's words won't leave me be. I *have* been afraid. Afraid of Pearl and the color of her skin. Afraid of my own skin. And even though I'm mad at Sophie for getting me into all this, I'm afraid of losing her and Mama and even Ellery. It seems to me that I've been afraid of losing people I love for so long I can't even remember what it's like not to feel that way. Maybe if I do this one thing tonight, I won't need to be afraid anymore. Maybe if I keep moving ahead like Fergus said, I'll know this for myself.

I straighten Fergus's cap on my head, take a deep breath and turn the Space Lander onto the footpath leading down to the Screaming River.

The path is shaded with weeping willows, and drapes of Spanish moss hang from the cypress trees. I would walk this path only for Fergus and Sophie. I think of them as I snap on the bike light and make my way through the shadows. I'm convinced that at any moment a spirit will jump out at me from those shadows, a hungry swamper looking for his evening meal, but I keep on walking.

It's here that they say those swampers died years ago, right here on the path. The water rose so quick and they were so drunk they couldn't scramble up the banks fast enough and got sucked right into the current and lost their lives. I can see how you could lose your footing in the dark, even if you were sober. The bank leading down to the water is steep and I have to lean my weight against the bike to keep it straight. Every once in a while a branch hits my face and it feels like a hand reaching out, trying to weave me into the vines. One of those ghostly branches grabs Fergus's cap off my head, but I'm not about to turn back for it now. I just keep moving steady until I can see a break in the moss and the moon peeks through.

There is no wind tonight and I'm trying to believe Mama's theory of the moaning being only wind, 'cause I don't have time to deal with ghosts. It is not a long path, for which I am grateful. As I emerge from the cypress grove, I can see the hill next to the church.

All I have to do is walk up that hill and I'll know if all of this has been a waste of time. I hear myself breathing hard and whispering under my breath with each step I take, pushing Ellery's bike in front of me. "Please God. Please God. Please God." Over and over along with the rhythm of the bike pedals turning on their own. I reach the crest of the hill and look down on the little white church. The windows of Screaming River Baptist are blazing with light.

✦ 11 ✦
Screaming River Baptist

I coast down the bumpy hill toward the bright windows of the church, get off Ellery's bike and lean it against the side of the Reverend Small's black Plymouth. I push open the doors of the church and everyone turns and looks. Some people jump, then smile. A few laugh with relief. Bertha Johnson motions me to her side. I walk down the aisle. Bertha gives me a big hug and scrambles around for a tissue in her pocket. I feel myself start to settle down inside.

The choir is standing up at the front of the church singing the last verse of "Ain't Gonna Let Nobody Turn Me 'Round." This must have been a spontaneous meeting, because the choir members are usually dressed in their very best for service, but tonight they're all wearing the same clothes they had on at the rally this morning.

When the choir finishes singing, Jake Henny walks up to the pulpit, clears his throat and looks directly at me.

"Miss Celli, do you have something to say to the congregation tonight?" Jake is tall and broad shouldered and has one of the deepest voices I've ever heard. Heads turn in a room whenever Jake speaks. Because of his big voice, he's always chosen to lead the service when the reverend is sick.

I realize that this is the first time I've been to church without Sophie. It feels funny, like I forgot to bring something important with me like my shoes. It must be what everyone else is feeling too, without the reverend there. Mrs. Small sits in the front row, looking kind of lost and frightened.

I guess I always thought that if I ever stood up before the congregation in this tiny church, I'd be all fancied up in my white cotton dress and my hair would be done in a bun. Instead I remember that my hair is tangled from the branches by the river and I'm wearing Ellery's dirty old sweatshirt that Fergus insisted would keep me from being seen on the road. I can just imagine what Sophie would say if she could see what I look like now. A wave of anger passes through me as I realize I wouldn't be here at all if it weren't for Sophie's love of trouble.

"Go ahead, Celli," Jake says. "Tell us what you come to say, now." My heart starts pounding.

"I've come to ask you for help getting Sophie out of jail. I'm all alone at my house and Ellery has been gone since sunup. My mama's in Atlanta and my grandma is in Vidalia."

Thelma Jackson and Bertha shake their heads and *tsk* under their breath. "Poor child," I hear Bertha say. I'm not sure if I should mention Fergus. I decide to keep quiet about it, because I notice there are folks in the congregation I don't know. Then I see Pearl's face among them and my heart pounds faster. I step down, still keeping my eyes on Pearl.

"Well, Celli," Jake says. "That's why we're all gathered here tonight—to make a plan to free the reverend, Sophie and everyone else from that prison cell."

Pearl stands up in the back row. "Sir, my name is Pearl and I came down with Manny O'Brien and the other Freedom Riders. I can stay with Celli until this is all worked out. I'm a friend of the family.

"Manny's been down at the jail all day. He's a good lawyer and can be real persuasive, so I think there's a chance Sophie and the reverend will be home in their own beds tonight." There's a buzz in the crowd.

"Now, that's good news, ma'am. Thank you." The congregation seems to relax at Pearl's words.

"Do you want to go home with your friend now, Celli?" he asks.

"Yes, sir," I say. "Thank you." But I don't feel thankful. My knees are shaking and my face is hot. I wonder if anyone knows who Pearl is? This might sound like a good solution to Jake Henny, but how can I accept Pearl's help when I haven't been very kind to her in my mind—I've been hoping she would just go back to Ohio and I'd never have to see her again.

Jake gestures for the congregation to rise. "Hymn number forty-five," he calls out and the ladies begin "Amazing Grace."

Pearl makes her way to the back door, where she stands waiting for me. I walk toward her, wondering what I'll say to her, when the sound of breaking glass fills the room and a bottle flies in through the window, hitting the front of the pulpit. Jake jumps back. It came mighty close to hitting his head.

The women in the choir stop singing and everyone gets down on the floor. Pearl grabs my hand and pulls me behind the last row of chairs, throwing herself over me and keeping my head down with her strong hand. She smells of soap and lavender. I am able to lift my head only enough to see a flaming bottle fly through the air and catch on to the curtain above Bertha's head. No one screams. Bertha grabs a vase of flowers off the pulpit and throws it at the curtains, quenching the fire. More bottles come through the windows all around us. It seems to go on forever and through it all is the sound of men's voices from outside and the banging of a hammer. I keep looking at the door, expecting it to open at any moment, but it doesn't.

Finally there is a screech of tires, the smell of smoke,

and then the room is silent, though I think I can hear everyone's heart beating as fast as my own.

We all slowly get up on our feet. Pearl dusts off the front of her dress. Jake marches to the back of the church and opens the door while the congregation follows. Out in the churchyard, maybe ten feet away, stands a flaming cross taller than Jake. The air smells heavy of gasoline. My stomach drops like a rock. By the light of the flames I can make out the smashed windshield of the reverend's car and a pair of shiny chrome handlebars lying on the ground. The Bowden Space Lander. Flat tires, twisted frame, as if a truck just backed over it.

I stare at the twisted heap lying before me and one question runs through my mind: Exactly how long will it take Ellery to kill me when he finds out?

A group of men disappear around the side of the church where the gardens are and come back dragging a hose and carrying several pairs of work gloves. Jake turns the nozzle and water sprays out, drenching the cross and extinguishing the flames. The men of the congregation put on the gloves and together they uproot the smoking cross and carry it back to the garden and the ladies kick ash around in the grass, as if they've done this a hundred times. Maybe they have.

Then the entire congregation gathers in a circle around the ashes and Ellery's bike. Pearl takes my right hand and Bertha takes my left and we finish singing "Amazing Grace."

✴ 12 ✴
Bail

"Come on in the kitchen," I say, holding the screen door open. A shaft of light from inside strikes the floor of the porch. Pearl nods her head. I hadn't really noticed before that she is a slight woman, very neat and trim. Her shoes match her hat. Her stockings are new, no snags or bumps. I've never seen a black woman in stockings. Things must be very different in Ohio.

When we're both in the kitchen, I close the door.

"May I use your phone, Celli? I need to call Manny. He's been at the jail all day. I want to reach him to see if there's any news." I nod my head and sit at the table, watching Pearl dial the number.

"May I please speak to Manny O'Brien?" Pearl asks. There is a long pause. "Hi, Manny. This is Pearl. I'm glad I caught you. Listen, has a woman named Sophie . . ." Pearl cups her hand over the receiver and turns to me. "Celli, what's Sophie's last name again?"

"Carter," I say.

"Sophie Carter been released yet?" Pause. "Mmmm. Really? That's awfully high. Are you sure? I see. Yes. I might be able to help you. I'm here with a young girl named Celli, who Sophie looks after. Sophie's needed here. What if Celli came down there and spoke on Sophie's behalf?" Pause. "I could bring her down." Pause. "All right, if you're sure. We'll wait, then. It's three-twenty-four Mariposa Drive. In about a half an hour. Fine. We'll be waiting. Thanks, Manny." Pearl gently places the phone on the hook. "Manny's sending someone over," she says, turning to me.

What's she talking about? Why do I have to go to the jailhouse? I've already done my part tonight. I thought Manny was the one who would get Sophie out, not me.

"Manny's having a hard time with Sophie. She refuses to go unless everyone is released, and the bail for her is set pretty high. I think if she knows you're there and are in need of her, she might change her mind. It's worth a try. Don't you think?"

"I don't want to go," I say, my face feeling hot.

"I know, Celli. But there is a better chance of Sophie coming home tonight if you go down there. You're her family, honey. She needs you."

"If she really needed me, she wouldn't be putting up

such a fuss. She would have come home the first chance she had."

I turn my back to Pearl and walk over to the sink, pour myself a glass of water. "I'm tired of being the only one who can help," I say.

"I'm not asking you to do it for me, Celli. You'd be doing it for Sophie. And you'd also be doing it for yourself. I imagine you'd rather have Sophie here watching after you instead of me. Am I right?" I turn around and face Pearl. I nod my head and she smiles.

"I just showed up here, Celli. I don't expect you or Ellery to accept me right off. Maybe you never will. You have a whole life that has nothing to do with me. I'm just a stranger to you." Pearl stops talking and watches me closely.

"All right," I say, looking down at my shoes. "I'll do it for Sophie. But it's the last thing I'm gonna do for her. She's just gotta stay out of trouble from now on."

Pearl smiles again and nods her head. She walks across the kitchen to the pantry, runs her fingers along the wood molding. She's silent for a long time and when she speaks again her voice is different—soft and kind of dreamy. "Your mama keeps a real fine house here, Celli," Pearl says. "Do you mind if I look around?" I shake my head. "Maybe you could give me a little tour? Might make us both more comfortable to walk around a bit." I lead Pearl to the dining room and the window seat.

"Oh, I like this," she says, settling herself on the cushions. "I always wanted to sit in a window and read. Is that what you do here?"

"Yes, ma'am."

"I bet your mama likes it here too. She was such a pretty young woman, though I never met her. I've only seen pictures."

"If you never met Mama, how did you ever meet Ellery and me?"

"Well, your daddy brought you both to the Macon Carnival one summer and I met him there. I wrote him saying how I had to see my grandchildren, even if it was just once. So he waited for me in front of the hot dog stand."

"Why did my daddy leave us?" The question is out of my mouth before I can stop myself.

Pearl looks out over my head into the wisteria vine on the other side of the window. I think maybe she can see the angels, but once they leave for the day they don't come back until the next. Pearl sighs.

"Your daddy lived in two worlds, Celli, and he never felt at home in either one of them. He passed for white, but he knew he was also black and that was too much for him to bear at times, so he did some drinking to forget his pain. I thought when he met your mama things would change.

"I wrote to your daddy once trying to convince him to move all of you up north, where the color of your skin doesn't matter quite so much, but he never did respond.

"He's still running from the pain, Celli, and that's bad, let me tell you. It would be better if he could turn around and face it, feel that pain through and through and be free from it instead of letting it eat him up inside."

Pearl sits for a moment, seeming a little stunned at what just came out of her. "I hope one day you can find your peace in both worlds, Celli."

I don't know what to say. I never knew it was like that for Daddy. I guess I always thought he left 'cause he was tired of us. I never thought of him as having any pain. I thought that was only for the ones who got left behind.

"Let's keep walking," Pearl says. I nod my head, but my mind is still trying to take in all she just told me.

We walk upstairs and I stop in my room to change out of my dark clothes and put on a plain cotton dress while Pearl waits for me in the hall. I stand in front of the mirror and run a comb through my hair, wipe a streak of dirt from my cheek. I open the top drawer of my bureau. Pearl's letter to Mama is in there, tucked beneath a handkerchief. Next to the letter is a tiny picture I have of Ellery holding Daddy's hand. That's really all you can see of Daddy in the photo—his hand and his left arm. Ellery gave it to me a long time ago 'cause he said he had other pictures of Daddy and him that were a whole lot better. I always used to wish that Daddy was holding my hand instead of Ellery's. I even tried to cover Ellery over in ink once, but it didn't help.

I was so little when Daddy left I don't remember the feel of him like Ellery does. I don't have anything I shared with him. No coins, no trains. But now I'm beginning to wonder if I do share something with him after all. Maybe Daddy gets that lonely feeling when the day is ending, just like I do.

I hear Pearl clear her throat and I put the photo back in the drawer and join her in the hall. We walk slowly downstairs, stopping at every photograph hung on the wall. Pearl seems to take in each one real deep, like she's trying to put together the last ten years. Like she'll never see it again so she's got to make a clear picture of it in her head. We both pause on the landing and stare at the photograph of Daddy holding Ellery when he was a baby. It's Ellery's favorite photo.

"Are you gonna tell Ellery who you are?" I ask, turning to Pearl.

"I was planning on it, Celli."

"Do you think I could talk to Mama first? It might be better if she told him. Ellery remembers Daddy in a certain way. I think it might be less of a shock if Mama tells him."

Pearl considers this for a moment and then nods her head. "If you think it's best, Celli, then I won't. But I would like to catch a glimpse of him before too long."

"I would too," I say as we make our way to the kitchen.

✦   ✦   ✦

"Well, honey, I guess we better get down to business. We don't want Sophie in that cell any longer than she has to be."

Pearl sits down at the kitchen table and opens up her pocketbook, takes out an envelope filled with cash. "Manny just told me that bail is set at five hundred dollars for Sophie. They probably would have set it even higher if they expected anyone to pay it." She pushes the envelope across the table to me.

"Down here, it's trickier. I don't want to scare you, honey, but sometimes they like to hold on to folks to teach the others a lesson. A black woman speaking out on the courthouse steps doesn't go over real big in a town like Mystic, and I hear Sophie has a bit of a reputation already." I nod my head.

Pearl tells me everything she knows about getting a black woman out of prison. I don't ask any questions about how she knows so much, but by the way she's talking I get the feeling she's been in one of those jail cells herself.

"One of the Freedom Riders will be here in a few minutes to drive you to the jailhouse. When you get there, you just follow Manny. He'll tell the officer on duty that you've come to post bail for Sophie.

"You say you've come to get Sophie. I'm sure they'll know who she is. Manny will tell the officer you're all alone here, your own mama is away in Atlanta, and Sophie is all you got to watch out for you. If they decide to let her go, they'll make you sign a piece of paper for her release. Read it over carefully and don't sign it unless it has Sophie's name printed on the top. Don't give them any money until after you sign it and they give you a copy. Just let Manny do all the talking. He's been getting folks out of jail longer than you've been alive."

A taxi pulls up in the driveway and from the window I can see the figure of a tall man get out and hand some money to the driver, close the door.

"There he is," Pearl says.

She straightens the collar on my dress and gives me a gentle push toward the door. My legs are so tired from the bike ride I feel like I have cement in my shoes.

Pearl greets a white man named Jonathan at the back door and gives him the keys to her car. She is just about to introduce me to him when I suddenly remember Fergus. I can't leave him in the basement while Pearl roams the house. What if she finds him? What if he hears her and comes out? I have to trust Pearl—and somehow, that isn't hard to do.

"I have a favor to ask of you before I go." Pearl nods her head. I walk over to the cellar door and give it three knocks. In a minute there are footsteps and the handle turns. Fergus emerges cautiously into the kitchen, squinting, trying to adjust his eyes to the light.

"Pearl, this is Fergus Freeman," I say, like it's the most natural thing in the world to have a black man in a dress hiding in my cellar. "Fergus, this here is Pearl. I think she's the best person to help you now." Pearl and Fergus stare at each other.

"Well, what do you know?" Pearl says, taking in Fergus's lumpy bosom. "Why don't you have a seat at the table here, Mister Freeman, and we can have a little talk while I fix up a good hot meal. I think we're all gonna need a good meal before this night is over, don't you?"

"Yes, ma'am," Fergus replies quietly.

"I hear the food in jail isn't very tasty these days," Pearl says.

"I hear that too," I say as I head out the door.

We arrive home at midnight. It took two hours to get Sophie free and there was no way I could have done it without Manny being there beside me, talking his sweet, smooth talk. Manny seems to have a way of making sense out of mixed-up situations. Flustered by the day's events, the officer on duty, Bud Lowry, got all twisted around in Manny's words and couldn't find any reason not to take five hundred dollars for Sophie's freedom.

"You tell your mama I'm glad to help her out just this once, but she's gonna have to keep a closer watch on her help." He gave me a wink and I felt like I might be sick.

After signing papers and talking more to Manny, he turned his back on us, picked a key from his chain and carried his heavy frame slowly down the hall to where they keep the prisoners. The hallway was painted lime green, with one bare lightbulb hanging by a wire overhead shining down on Bud Lowry's bald spot, making a big shadow of him along the floor.

From the moment we walked through the front door of the jailhouse until Bud Lowry left to get Sophie, there were two sounds that filled the room. The whir of an electric fan in the window over the officer's desk and the low hum of voices singing "We Shall Overcome" from inside and out. Manny and I had to walk through a whole pack of Freedom Riders on our way into the jail and the sound of their singing sent the small hairs on the back of my neck standing straight out. Manny told me they'd been there all day. It seems Bud Lowry only had enough jail cells for a handful of the rowdier protesters. Those not jailed took their places outside, singing and holding candles and signs. Folks patted us on the back as we walked through, like we were heroes or something. I didn't feel much like a hero. I just wanted to free Sophie and get on home.

After ten minutes Officer Lowry came back down the hall with Sophie. She was walking with her head held high.

"This is the first time she's stopped talking all day long. A trouble nigger is what she is." My stomach gripped tight at the word and my fists clenched. Manny reached his hand down and covered my fist until it softened.

"I think she's learned her lesson today, ain't you, auntie?" Sophie was silent. I could see her wince and I wasn't sure if it was because he called her auntie or 'cause the gash over her left eye was giving her pain. Officer Lowry told her if he ever saw her talking in front of a crowd of people again, she'd end up sitting in that jail cell for the rest of her days. Told her he'd be watching her close to make sure she stayed quiet.

I gave the keys to Sophie and we said goodbye to Manny at the door. He was staying on. "Reverend Small won't leave until everyone is let out," Manny told us, and Sophie nodded her head.

"That's right. I wouldn't expect any less from that man. I tell you, if he weren't already married, I'd marry him myself. He knows they don't like to keep a preacher overnight. God bless him and God bless you, Mister O'Brien," Sophie said, shaking Manny's hand.

"You better move along, auntie." Bud Lowry's voice echoed down the corridor. "You better get home now before I change my mind."

I could barely stand there and watch that man talk to Sophie in the hard way he had while Sophie said nothing. I got to feeling real scared, like something had happened to her, but as soon as we were closed tight inside Pearl's car with the doors locked, Sophie started laughing.

"Did you hear that ignorant white man? Who does he think he is calling me auntie? Do I look like his auntie? Do I look like a big old white woman? Lord, I had to do everything I could to keep myself from calling him some names God would never forgive me for saying."

"How come you didn't?" I asked. There was an edge to my voice and I figured I was about ready to cry or yell. Sophie turned to me.

"Why, honey, that man was just about pushed past his limit. He's scared of all us strong black folk right now. If I spoke my mind, then that man would never leave me alone. Come visit me some dark night all dressed in his white sheets, burning crosses on my lawn. I have to bide my time so I can fight another day."

I folded my arms across my chest and looked down at the floor of the car.

"You've had a long day, now, haven't you, Celli?"

I thought that after everything that had happened I would have been glad just to see Sophie alive, but I found myself burning up with anger toward her. "What do you think, Sophie?" I asked, all filled with spit.

"I think you did, missy, and don't use that tone with me. Just 'cause I been gone for one day don't give you the right to talk bad to me."

"You don't know what I've been through tonight, Sophie. You have no idea where I've been." Then the words ran right out of me like a river. "If you weren't involved with this stupid Movement, I wouldn't be here right now getting you out of jail. I wouldn't have been at the Screaming River Church tonight with the Klan throwing fire bottles through the windows. And I'd have a few friends left whose mothers wouldn't be afraid to invite me into their houses. If you could just keep quiet for once, Sophie, and know your place, maybe I could have a normal life."

Sophie sat up taller in her seat. "You think this is all

about *you*? Is that what you think? You think because you were inconvenienced tonight, I should stop speaking the truth. You got to wake up, girl! This isn't about you. This is bigger than you. It's bigger than any of us. Can't you see that? My people have a chance to take back their power, their dignity. Nothing is more important to me than that, Celli. Nothing. Do you understand?" I nodded my head. Tears welled up in my eyes and Sophie's, too.

"I'm just tired of worrying about you, Sophie. I worry about you every day. All the time. I thought they killed you today. I thought you were never coming home. Not ever." Sophie wiped a tear from my cheek.

"We all get tired, honey," she said, folding me into her arms. "But we can't give up. Not now."

⋆ 13 ⋆
The Cap

The house is all lit up and the smell of fried chicken drifts out into the night. I'm not sure what Sophie's going to think of another woman cooking in her kitchen, but she doesn't seem to mind.

"Mighty nice of you to help us tonight, ma'am," is all she says. I think Sophie is just glad to be home. She sits down at the table next to Fergus and fusses over his dress while he tells her what happened to him today.

"What are we gonna do with you, honey?" Sophie asks, running her hand over the top of his head. "Why, that dress just doesn't suit you at all."

Fergus smiles. "I left it on, Sophie, in case someone were to come here looking for me." He glances over at Pearl, who clears her throat.

"Fergus and I have been getting acquainted here tonight and I've been thinking, Sophie, that maybe I should take Fergus with me back to Ohio for a time, until all this blows over."

Sophie nods her head slowly. I can tell she's real sad at the thought of Fergus leaving. But there is no more talk about it just now. We all sit down at the table, everyone but Ellery. Nobody says anything. We just eat. We eat like there hasn't been food in the world for a month. It's the most delicious food I've ever had, even better than Sophie's. Fried chicken and potato salad. Sophie and I have second helpings. Fergus is the only one who can't seem to finish his plate. He pushes his potatoes around in a circle and looks out the window every time a car turns the corner from Sibly Drive onto Mariposa.

I'm just putting down my fork and wiping my face with a napkin when there is a movement outside the window and Fergus ducks under the table. It's Ellery sneaking up the driveway. I can see his shadow against the cherry tree. He's trying to find another way in besides the back door. Sophie sees him too. A wave of guilt comes over me as I think about Ellery's bike. He left it this afternoon all shiny and new and now it's in Pearl's trunk, the handlebars twisted, the tires flat, covered in road dust.

"Mister Ellery, you get your sneaky, no-shame self in here this minute," Sophie yells out the window.

Fergus slides up into his chair with a sigh of relief and Ellery slinks through the door, standing with his back up against the screen, not sure if he's gonna have to run for it out into the night or stay. As he comes into the light of the kitchen, Pearl gasps. Ellery's right cheek is swollen and bruised. His lip is bleeding and his shirt is half torn from his back.

"Well, what sorry mess have you gotten yourself into this time?" Sophie asks, dampening a dishcloth, walking over to Ellery and dabbing it on his lip to stop the bleeding. Ellery studies the gash over Sophie's eye, then catches sight of Fergus and stares at him as if he's seeing a ghost.

"I swear, child, you ain't got enough brains to tan your own hide," Sophie says, pushing Ellery into a chair. "Sit down. Where in heaven have you been?"

Ellery's lip is all fat from the cut and his words come out kind of muffled. I can see tracks of dried tears on his dirty face. "I been out with Shelby," he says.

"Mmm-hmm," Sophie says, waiting for more of an explanation. Ellery squirms in his chair, looking at Pearl, who he's never seen before. We don't get many strangers coming over to visit this time of night.

"I didn't think anyone would miss me today, and Shelby's mama thought he was at my house." Ellery hesitates. "We jumped a freight to Macon. Shelby wanted to buy a model airplane at Reynolds and I needed a part for my bike. We missed the 6:05 train and had to wait for the 8:25 back and it was late, so we didn't get to Mystic till after dark." Ellery pauses and takes a sip of water from a cup Sophie is holding out for him.

"Did you fall off the train or something, Ellery? What happened to your face?" I ask.

"No, I did not fall off the train," Ellery says, looking at me like I have no brains at all. "We were walking home along the river and I found Fergus's cap washed up on the bank." He pulls a soggy black cap from his back pocket and places it on the table.

"We ran into Ned and Jimmy Bottle coming up the path behind the Methodist church. They were looking for Fergus. Jimmy told us Fergus broke Wallace's window and that his daddy was gonna lynch Fergus when he found him. Ned wanted Shelby and me to help them, but I said we couldn't. I said we had other things to do." Ellery glances over at Fergus.

"They grabbed Fergus's cap out of my hands, asking me if it wasn't the Jew-boy's cap. I wouldn't say, so they started calling me names. Said my mama and little sister loved Negroes, so I probably did too. Then they took turns hitting me and Shelby ran." Ellery reaches up and takes Sophie's hand from his cheek. "That hurts, Sophie. Leave me be." Sophie hands Ellery the dishcloth and sits down next to Pearl.

"Jimmy threw the cap at me and wanted to know why it was all wet, so I told him I found it at the edge of the river. Then he said he knew where Fergus Freeman was now, thanks to me. Washed down the river. He laughed and said I could kiss that no-account half-breed goodbye forever." Ellery pushes the cap toward Fergus and we all stare at it.

"On my way home, I heard people talking. Jimmy's got a big mouth, so I guess by now the entire town thinks Fergus drowned. I heard someone say that the way the current was moving his body might be all the way to Vidalia by now. They called off the search."

We all look over at Fergus and a smile spreads across his face. "The Lord does work in mighty mysterious ways," he says, passing his plate to Pearl for an extra helping of chicken.

✦ ✦ ✦

After supper, while everyone is getting properly acquainted, the telephone rings. It's Mama home from her picnic. *Kind of late for a picnic,* I think. Sophie speaks to her first.

"Hi, honey . . . Sure . . . We're just fine. We're having a late supper here with a friend." There's a pause. "No, no one you know, sugar. Just someone we met passing through town and took a liking to." Sophie looks over at us. Pause.

"Why, they're fine as fudge. Growing like weeds. I can hardly keep track of 'em, they're moving around so fast these days." Pause. "Sure, she's right here." Sophie hands me the phone and gives me a look. I know this look. This look means tell Mama only good news. Sophie will tell

Mama all the rest when she gets home, but for now, Sophie wants Mama to enjoy her vacation.

"Hi, Mama," I say quietly.

"Hi, Celli. Etta said you called. Is everything okay? I've been trying to reach you all evening." All the feelings that have been jumping up and down inside of me today settle themselves into one—a deep longing at the sound of Mama's voice.

"Sure, Mama. Everything is fine. I just missed you today."

"I miss you too, honey. I went on a picnic this afternoon. It was such a beautiful day here. I picked some honeysuckle. It smelled so sweet." Mama's voice sounds all high and airy.

"That's nice," I say. "I wish I'd been with you today, Mama, picking flowers. Are you having a good time?"

"I've never had such a good time. I can hardly wait to tell you all about it. I'll be home end of the week. I love you, Celli."

"I love you, too, Mama."

"Is Ellery there?"

"Yes, ma'am. I'll put him on. Good night, Mama," I whisper, trying to keep my tears back. I hand the phone to Ellery, who is glad to have a distraction from Sophie and Pearl's fussing.

When Ellery hangs up the phone, Pearl offers another round of huckleberry pie and Fergus holds out his plate. He seems like a completely different person, like the weight of the world has been lifted from his shoulders. Sophie, too, is on her third piece of pie. I can tell she is impressed with Pearl's cooking.

"Where did you learn to cook, girl?" Sophie asks.

"Same place you did." Pearl answers. "In my mama's kitchen."

Sophie laughs and nods her head. Pearl is old enough to be Sophie's mama. But Sophie always seems to be the oldest, no matter who she's talking to.

"I know this sweet boy is gonna be in good hands, then," Sophie says, running her hand over Fergus's head.

✶ 14 ✶
Birthday Cake

Mama is due home tomorrow. The temperature has gone above one hundred degrees and the peppers are wilting on the vine. Sophie made me go out and pick all of them so as not to lose any in the heat. She'll make sweet-potato-and-pepper corn cakes for my birthday dinner tomorrow. She also sent me down to the Humdinger to pick up five pounds of flour, a pound of sugar and a can of cocoa. She didn't say what for, but I'm beginning to guess, as there has been no mention of dragging the ice cream maker down from the garage and washing it out. Even though she won't come out and say it, I know she's proud of what I did for her and Fergus. Proud enough to break tradition.

"Celli, go down to the cellar and bring up the sheets in the basket, hang them on the line."

I'm glad to do it. The cellar is cool, the only place in the house I want to be. I take my time walking down the steps, sit on the bottom one in the dampness. The cellar is dirt floor, spiderwebs in the windows, half slices of green light streaming in from the kudzu-lined panes.

I haven't been down here since before Fergus hid out two days ago. Seems longer than that. Sophie says this has been one of the longest weeks of her life and I have to say the same.

Since everyone in Mystic is convinced Fergus drowned in the Screaming River, getting him out of town wasn't too difficult. He and Pearl slept at our house that night and after breakfast the next day, Pearl backed her Rambler up to the porch. She made Fergus get into the trunk with her suitcase, just to be on the safe side.

Fergus thanked me for losing his cap and Ellery for finding it. I tied his purple ribbon around his index finger so he'd remember he wasn't alone.

Pearl took me aside for a moment and told me how proud she was to have met me. "Maybe one day," she said, "we could spend some more time together. If you like." I nodded my head.

"Thank you, Pearl," I said. "For helping us last night."

"I was glad to, Celli. It's not often I get a chance to help out such a fine family," she said, and smiled.

"You smile just like Daddy did," I said, remembering

the photo of him on the mirror over my bureau. Pearl pulled me toward her and hugged me tight.

"Thank you, Celli," she said. "I think you're right about that."

When everyone had said their goodbyes, Sophie handed Pearl a large bag of fried chicken and biscuits and then Pearl checked one last time on Fergus and closed the trunk. She got into her lime green Rambler and drove down Mariposa, heading north toward the county line.

We haven't heard from either of them since they left. Sophie says they're probably still on the road. She says she has a real good feeling about them and I'm beginning to agree with her, cause I have that good feeling too. Sophie doesn't know who Pearl really is. I didn't tell her. It still feels too new and tender to share with anyone besides Mama.

The basket of sheets is on top of our new Sears washing machine. Sophie wanted to put the machine in the kitchen, as it is such a pretty thing and easier for her than walking up and down the stairs, but Mama insists that washing machines belong in the basement out of sight. She said she read in one of her fashion magazines that that's how women do it these days, keep all the dirty laundry in the basement.

"That figures," says Sophie. "That just shows you what white folk have to worry themselves over. How things look on the outside. Don't want nobody knowing they got dirty underwear or socks with enough sweat in them they could walk down the street on their own, just like everybody else. No, the white folk got to be above the rest. Got to be perfect in their imperfect world. Got to keep their washing machines hidden in the basement." Ellery and I roll our eyes at each other when Sophie starts talking on like that.

The laundry basket is filled to the brim with Ellery's bedsheets and my overalls, a couple of Sophie's aprons. There is something white sticking out of the pocket in the front of the overalls. I pull it out. A soggy folded piece of paper, all wadded together from the soap and water, the ink gone a light shade of green. My letter from Pearl. I can't believe I left it in there, didn't put it away somewhere safe. I can only make out a few words, *I will be . . . your grandma . . . when you were very young.* The rest have bled into the paper itself. I remember the day that letter came and how I thought it meant I'd be meeting my daddy soon.

I feel sad thinking about Daddy never knowing which world to live in. But somehow I understand him better than I did before I met Pearl. I understand that pain Pearl was talking about, because it's inside of me. I hope I don't get stuck between black and white the way Daddy did. Like Pearl said, maybe I can find my peace being both.

Sophie's voice filters down through the floorboards, her sentences broken by the whir of the electric mixer just like the sentences in my letter.

"Celli, what . . . doing? . . . slow as molasses . . . don't have all day . . ." I take the wad of paper and put it into the pocket of my dress, walk up the steps and emerge into the heat and light of the kitchen.

"I thought you got swallowed up by that pretty new washing machine." Sophie shakes the beater into the bowl. Chocolate frosting.

"What are you doing, Sophie?" I ask, dipping my finger into the bowl, licking off the sweetness.

"None of your business, missy. Go hang them sheets." Sophie gives me a wink. Her eye is healing up just fine.

I haven't seen the angels since the night they found Sophie's ribbon in the grass, but as I walk to the laundry line I see the shimmer of their wings on the roof of the garage. From this distance it looks like they're drinking soda pop and playing a game. Dealing out cards. Five for each. Poker. I never thought angels played poker. I never thought angels were black or my size. I never thought I'd be so lucky as to ever see one for real.

I wish there was a way to thank them for reminding me that I'm not alone in the world. I'd write them a letter if I thought they could read it, but somehow I don't think they could. I think the language of angels doesn't have any written form. It comes directly from the heart.

In the evening Sophie places my cake on the windowsill to cool and wraps the frosting tight with foil, balancing it on top of the pickled okra she has fermenting in the fridge. I sure hope it doesn't fall in and mix together. Frosting is my favorite part.

We will have a small party, just family. Usually Katie comes, but I don't think she will this year. She's been spending a lot of time with Vale Austin these days. I wave when I see them playing hopscotch, but Katie just picks up her stones and crosses to the other side of the street so she won't have to strike up a conversation with me.

I asked Sophie if Tilly and Rosa could come to my party instead, even though it isn't on a Sunday, and Sophie said she'd ask Bertha for me.

Ellery is out in the garage, hammering away at something. He won't let me near. In fact, he has permanently banned me from the garage. He took the news of the Space Lander pretty hard, wouldn't talk to me for a whole day. I wasn't sure if he'd ever forgive me, but this morning he told me that since I'm a girl he's not surprised I'd do such a stupid thing. These are the most understanding words Ellery has ever spoken to me.

The sun is dipping low over the roof of the barn. The angels collect their cards and fly off in the fading light. Sophie calls me onto the porch and pulls out the quilt. We've been too busy with all the commotion of the past week to work on it, so it's not finished yet, but Mama will get the idea. I can't believe it's taken shape considering we started with one crooked square three weeks ago. It's real pretty. Twelve squares stitched together. Each one is a separate scene. One of Ellery by the railroad tracks. One of Sophie cooking in the kitchen. Maypops and sweet-brier bordered with wisteria. Freedom Riders looking out the windows of a bus. And me kneeling in the garden, gazing up at the barn roof. All pieced together out of Ellery's old pajama bottoms and dresses I've grown out of. Sophie did most of the work. I only helped stitch it together.

"You know, Sophie, this square is missing something," I say, pointing to the one of me looking at the barn roof. She bends over my shoulder.

"What's it missing, honey?"

I pull Sophie's purple ribbon from my pocket. She watches me and for once doesn't say anything. I pull out a section of purple thread from Sophie's sewing basket, thread a needle and start stitching the ribbon above the roof of the barn. "So we'll always remember we're never alone," I say. Then I sit back in the rocking chair and tell Sophie a story about angels.

Epilogue

It's been one whole year since the "summer of angels," as Sophie likes to call it. I turned twelve just like I expected to and Mama came home right before the slicing of the first birthday cake I ever had. Sophie frosted the cake and on the top she perched a tiny black ceramic angel that Reverend Small gave her after choir practice one week. The reverend is still sending his praises up to heaven at full volume, holding services on Sunday, and mass meetings on Wednesday nights in his tiny box of a church, and his silent wife serves pie to the faithful when he's done with them to bring them back to the land of the living.

The congregation at Screaming River Baptist took the

passing of Fergus real hard until Sophie explained that he wasn't really gone at all. Only relocated.

The rest of Mystic, however, believes that Fergus Freeman drowned in the Screaming River that night, and that has divided the town in a different way. You see, the truth eventually came out, as Sophie said it always does. Laud Spigget's brother Hank threw the rock through the front window of Wallace's Five-and-Dime to scare the Freedom Riders who were sitting at the lunch counter, and Fergus just happened to be standing nearby, like he told me.

When the town matrons found out Fergus was innocent, they got all fired up. Many of them refused to speak to their husbands for quite some time. Mrs. Adler held a small memorial service at St. James, the big white church in the center of town. She dedicated a plaque in memory of Fergus Freeman in hopes that such a senseless tragedy would not happen again. Some folks agree with her, but there are others who are only too glad to be rid of one more black man in this town and it might be a long time before that way of thinking changes.

I'd like to say that the town of Mystic, Georgia, is at peace now, but that isn't true. The day after the rally, all the Freedom Riders piled into the one bus that hadn't been burned and drove out of Mystic, leaving a big cloud of dust, which hasn't settled yet. Sophie says she hopes it never settles. She says that the best thing that could have happened did. The town of Mystic got shaken up.

"That's the first step, Celli," she told me. "The white folks got a little uncomfortable last summer and maybe a few of them woke up. Now we just gotta wake up the rest." Sophie says maybe that's how change starts. One or two folks letting go of the way they thought things should be and opening their minds to a different way. Maybe even one person willing to change is something to celebrate.

The Freedom Riders continued on into Alabama and Mississippi, with Manny O'Brien leading them. Reverend Small says that even though not much has changed in Mystic, there is now a law protecting black and white folks sitting beside one another on buses in the South. So all the Freedom Riders' hard work and courage paid off after all.

Sophie went back to her small house for the fall and winter to care for Granny Rose, who ended up in the churchyard before spring, next to Sophie's mama and papa. Sophie wears black these days, but she's still talking up a storm, even in her grief.

The quilt Sophie and I made hangs on the wall over Mama's bed. Mama asked me the meaning of the purple ribbon above the barn roof and I told her it was my idea. "Like an angel," I said. "Watching over us." She smiled and tilted her head, trying to understand my meaning.

Sophie says this summer is gonna be real different from last. "We're gonna keep it quiet," she says. Though knowing Sophie, that's hard to imagine. If anything, Sophie's day in jail made her bolder than ever. One Wednesday a month when the reverend goes to Atlanta on church business, she leads the mass meeting at Screaming River. Since the meetings are always on a school night, I have yet to attend one, but I've been told they get loud enough to shake the rafters and often go on half the night. The congregation is planning another rally for this July, so I guess there's a lot to shake the rafters about.

Though I still worry about her, I know Sophie is doing what she has to do and the Lord is watching over her.

Mama came home from Aunt Etta's with a strong passion for painting on canvas, picnics and a man named Sampson. Sophie teases Mama about Sampson, because unlike the Sampson in the Bible, Mama's Sampson has almost no hair to speak of, just a few blond wisps to comb over the top of his head. Sampson comes down from Atlanta once a week to take Mama out to dinner or to the movies. Even though he's nothing like what I imagine my daddy to be, Mama seems all wound around his heart, which I think might be more long-lasting than his lips, which are mighty thin.

Mama is planning her next trip to Atlanta, though she says she might come home early 'cause she missed out on too much here last summer. Sophie told her about everything that went on while she was gone.

I gave Mama Pearl's letter that I'd been keeping in my bureau and I told Mama all about her. She took a deep breath when I was done.

"I didn't even know about your daddy's color in the beginning, Celli. You'd never guess by looking at him. He was as light as you or Ellery. You've seen the pictures. He never once talked about family and I just figured he didn't have any. But one day while I was spring cleaning, I came across a picture of his mama and daddy and he told me everything. He made me promise never to tell a soul, so I never did, not even you kids or Grandma Flo. After moving back to Mystic, I especially didn't want anyone to know. I didn't want to make it harder for you than it already was. You know what Fergus's life was like here. But I'm glad you know now. I'm glad you met Pearl."

Both Pearl and Fergus are settled in Cleveland now. We get a letter every couple of months telling us of their adventures. Fergus wrote us a few lines about crossing the Ohio River. He said he knew how the slaves who crossed before him must have felt. He's a real free man now.

Mama told Ellery the whole story about Pearl and Daddy and that same day he took the picture of John Wayne down off the wall above his workbench and threw it away. I guess he figured there are some things John Wayne can't help him with anymore, like how to make peace with the family he has.

Ellery has been spending more time with Chester lately, washing him and combing out his shaggy fur. Sophie says that if Ellery is willing to spend time with that dirty beast, then either he has a high fever or something inside him is changing. I'm not sure which it is.

All I know is my presence doesn't seem to annoy Ellery anymore and he doesn't bother me half as much as he used to.

For my birthday, Ellery untwisted the wrecked Space Lander, dusted it off and lowered the seat for me. He said it wasn't good enough to enter in the Macon Carnival in August, so I might as well have it while he works on the Space Lander II for next year.

I still glance at myself whenever I pass the hall mirror, looking for some sign that I'm different, but I look pretty much the same. My skin is no darker than it was. My eyes are still blue. But I feel different on the inside. I'm not as afraid about losing people and things changing as I used to be. And even the idea of Pearl and Daddy's color being part of me doesn't seem as strange as it once did. I'm beginning to see that life doesn't always turn out the way you think it will. And that's not necessarily bad. Sometimes when it all shakes out, you're left with something pretty good after all.

And the angels? I haven't seen them since my birthday. I cut a big wedge of cake for them and placed it beneath the willow tree. They sat in the branches looking down at me as I laid the plate in the grass, letting me get closer to them than ever before. As I backed away they waved and blew kisses in my direction, and the smallest angel scooped a handful of dust from a pouch hanging around her wrist and sprinkled some in my hair. They must have liked Sophie's cake, 'cause when I went out in the evening even the plate was gone.

I think the angels had somewhere else to go for now, someone else to help, but maybe they'll be back. Sophie says once you have angels with you they never ever go away.

Author's Note

Stories often begin for me with an opening sentence, and *Black Angels* was no exception. "I believe in angels, black angels . . ." came to me after a dream of three black angels. I put that sentence down on paper, eager to learn more, and the rest of the story came.

I was born three years after *Black Angels* takes place, so I never witnessed the events of the civil rights movement. I grew up in the white suburbs of upstate New York, far away from Georgia and the struggles of the people there. But I remember hearing stories about Dr. Martin Luther King at a very young age and though I can't really explain it, I have always felt a strong connection to that time and place.

What I know about Georgia in 1961 has been gathered

from a variety of sources: documentaries, movies, conversations and stories in books—specifically, *Freedom's Children: Young Civil Rights Activists Tell Their Own Stories* by Ellen Levine. And most importantly, I discovered the summer of 1961 through the characters of Celli and Sophie, whose story insisted on being told.

I believe in angels and I also believe that stories wait patiently, hanging around the fringes of our activity in search of someplace to land or someone sitting quietly at a desk willing to listen. I am grateful that I happened to be listening when Celli began her story.

In the summer of 1961, the civil rights movement was gaining strength in small towns in the south. Black and white volunteers known as Freedom Riders rode side by side on buses and ate at whites-only lunch counters, risking their lives to protest the injustice of segregation.

The Freedom Rides were some of the most successful nonviolent protests of the civil rights movement, ending victoriously in November 1961 when the United States government declared the integration of interstate bus stations. In the years to follow, many civil rights workers were honored with the title of Freedom Rider.

The word *nigger* is used in this book sparingly. Like Celli, I, too, feel like I want to "wipe off all the grime of that word that has settled on my skin" whenever I have heard it used. The word represents to me all the fear and ignorance of those unwilling to consider another way. Therefore, I left it in the mouths of characters in the book who represent those qualities. These same characters use the word *Jew* in a derogatory way.

Sometimes my characters say things that make me uncomfortable, but I have to honor their way of telling their own story. *Black Angels* takes place in a time of painful change in the American South, where some people chose fear and violence and others, like Sophie, chose courage.

About the Author

Rita Murphy lives in Vermont with her husband and son. Her first novel, *Night Flying,* won the 1999 Delacorte Press Prize for a First Young Adult Novel.